His lip curled into a sneer, tugging at the scar tissue on his cheek. "Is this the man you want in your bed at night? For the rest of your life?"

Her eyes went then not to his face, but to his hands. Large hands, wide and square, they bore scars, too. But they also looked as if they possessed strength, confidence. The images in her mind were quick and hot, dark hands on pale skin.

Katharine's body heated from the inside out, warmth pooling in her stomach and spreading slowly through her. The way he said it was intended to sound like a threat, but his deep, smooth voice made it sound like a promise. Rather than repel her, it fascinated her, on a level she didn't quite understand. No, he didn't frighten her, but that feeling did. Foreign and strong, filling her with adrenaline and languor at the same time, weakness and strength.

She didn't know how it had happened. How simple words had affected her like that. She threw it off, pushed ahead. She wasn't here to be intimidated— she was here to get what she needed. "There is an agreement."

**MAISEY YATES** knew she wanted to be a writer even before she knew what it was she wanted to write.

At her very first job she was fortunate enough to meet her very own tall, dark and handsome hero, who happened to be her boss, and promptly married him and started a family. It wasn't until she was pregnant with her second child that she found her very first Harlequin Presents® book in a local thrift store—and by the time she'd reached the happily ever after, she had fallen in love. She devoured as many as she could get her hands on after that, and she knew that these were the books she wanted to write.

She started submitting, and nearly two years later, while pregnant with her third child, she received The Call from her editor. At the age of twenty-three she sold her first manuscript to the Harlequin Presents line, and she was very glad that the good news didn't send her into labor!

She still can't quite believe she's blessed enough to see her name on not just any book, but on her favorite books.

Maisey lives with her supportive, handsome, wonderful, diaper-changing husband and three small children, across the street from her parents and the home she grew up in, in the wilds of southern Oregon. She enjoys the contrast of living in a place where you might wake up to find a bear on your back porch, then walking into the home office to write stories that take place in exotic, urban locales.

# HAJAR'S
# HIDDEN LEGACY

## MAISEY YATES

~ Beasts of the Desert ~

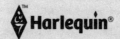

TORONTO NEW YORK LONDON
AMSTERDAM PARIS SYDNEY HAMBURG
STOCKHOLM ATHENS TOKYO MILAN MADRID
PRAGUE WARSAW BUDAPEST AUCKLAND

Recycling programs
for this product may
not exist in your area.

ISBN-13: 978-0-373-52877-6

HAJAR'S HIDDEN LEGACY

Copyright © 2012 by Maisey Yates

This edition published by arrangement with Harlequin Books S.A.

For questions and comments about the quality of this book please contact us at Customer_eCare@Harlequin.ca.

® and TM are trademarks of the publisher. Trademarks indicated with ® are registered in the United States Patent and Trademark Office, the Canadian Trade Marks Office and in other countries.

www.Harlequin.com

Printed in U.S.A.

# HAJAR'S
# HIDDEN LEGACY

For Ellie—there's nothing quite as special as a friend who has always been there, and who always will be. You're that friend for me.

# CHAPTER ONE

THEY called him the Beast of Hajar for a reason. Katharine could see that now. Zahir S'ad al Din was every bit as frightening as they said. He was an entirely different man from the one she'd met so many years ago. Cold, completely forbidding.

But Katharine didn't have the luxury of being frightened by him. Anyway, she was used to cold, forbidding men.

"Sheikh Zahir," she began, taking a step toward his expansive desk. He wasn't looking at her, his dark head inclined, his focus on a paper in front of him. "I have been waiting for you to contact me. You haven't."

"No, I have not. Which makes me wonder why you are here."

Katharine swallowed. "To marry you."

"Is that right, Princess Katharine? I had heard a rumor about that, but I didn't believe it." He lifted his head and for the first time, Katharine saw his face.

Yes, he was every bit as frightening as they said. The skin on the left side of his face ravaged, his eye not as focused or sharp on that side. Yet she still felt like he was seeing all the way into her, as if the accident that had served to cloud his physical vision had made him able to see more than a mere mortal man.

That he was a ghost, or a god of some kind was part of his legend, and looking at him now, she understood why.

"I did call." She hadn't exactly talked to Zahir, but she'd talked to his advisor. And she hadn't really been invited, either.

"I didn't think you would travel all the way from the comfort of your palace to have your marriage proposal turned down, as I was certain I had relayed my thoughts on the matter."

She straightened her shoulders. "I thought you owed me a conversation. A personal one, not your relayed response. And I didn't come to be turned down. I came to make sure the contract was honored. The deal was struck six years ago…"

"For you to marry Malik. Not me."

Thinking of Malik always made her feel sad. But her sadness was for a young life cut short, nothing deeper. He had been her destiny, her duty, for all of her adult life, and while she had liked him, cared for him in some ways, she had not loved him.

At first it seemed like losing him had changed everything, that her horizons had opened, that she might have a different future before her. It was clear now that nothing had changed.

Instead of Malik, it would be Zahir. But she was still destined to be sold into marriage for the sake of her country. She'd accepted it. Ultimately she hadn't felt that the change in groom had mattered all that much.

Although, looking at him now it became a whole different matter than it had been in theory. He was…he was something much more than she'd counted on.

*This was never about you. Never about your feelings. You have to be prepared to see this through.*

"That's what I thought. But when I examined the documents a little bit closer…" Her father had handled most of the legal portion of the marriage agreement that had been drawn up between her and Malik.

It hadn't really been of personal interest to her. Her relationship with him had been nothing more than political maneuvering by their parents. She'd only met him on a few occasions. She'd simply accepted that it was what she could do for her country, that the marriage was what she could contribute. She had never personally studied the agreement.

Until recently.

"Well, yes. But really, if you look at the wording, I am promised to Malik. Unless he is not able to assume the throne of Hajar. In that case, it is his successor that I'm meant to marry. That's you."

So strange to be standing before him, all but begging him to marry her when a large part of herself wanted to run out of the room. She didn't want to marry him, not on a personal level, any more than he wanted to marry her.

But her father was dying. Far too soon, and that put everything on a tight timetable. Her marriage had been pushed to some far off, fuzzy future after Malik's death, and for a while, no one had bothered her about it. For a while she had been allowed to serve in more of a practical manner, visiting the sick in hospitals, doing vital networking to bring more tourism dollars into the country. It had been liberating in a way, to find some use for herself outside of her gender and appearance.

But that time was over.

Her father only had a few months left, and Alexander, her brother and future king, didn't reach the legal age to rule for another six years. That meant someone had to be appointed Regent in the event of her father's death, and she lacked the necessary physical equipment to be considered.

She was over being bitter about that. Now she was ready to act.

If she didn't have a husband when her father died, the man placed in charge of her country would be her closest male relative. And what her closest male relative would do with that kind of power didn't even bear thinking about. She couldn't let it happen.

More than that, she had sworn to her father it would not happen. That she would secure the alliance with Hajar and the marriage to Zahir. That she would protect Alexander.

Failure was not an option. She couldn't look her father in the eye and tell him that she'd failed. She was a woman, and in the eyes of the authorities of her country, it made her subpar. In the eyes of her father, it seemed to have the same effect. Her father pushed her harder, demanded more and praised her less than he did Alexander. He saw Alexander's worth as a given; part and parcel to being the only male child. And Katharine had to work and work to prove she possessed any.

And she had welcomed it. She had been up to the challenge, always, to be all that she could be. To serve her family, her country and her people. A good thing, since she was the only hope left.

She wouldn't trip now, not in this last leg of the race. The thought of it made her insides tremble with sickness and dread. It made Zahir look friendly in comparison.

"I do not want a wife," he said, looking down again, obscuring his face from her view.

She crossed her arms beneath her breasts and tilted her chin up. "I didn't say I wanted a husband. This isn't about want. This is about need. About doing what is best for both of our countries. This marriage will strengthen the economy for both nations and whether it's Malik or…you…it doesn't change that it's the right thing to do."

Her words were cold. Mercenary. They chilled her to the bone. And yet she had to do this. For the lives of her people, the future of a nation.

Anyway, it wasn't as though she was sacrificing herself on the altar. Though in many ways she might be termed the Virgin Sacrifice.

The thought made her shudder. She would never be that. This was her choice. No one had forced her into Zahir's office. If she wanted to stand back and watch her country go to hell while she partied in Europe, there was nothing to stop her from doing it. Nothing except common decency, a sense of what was right. Nothing but the need to prove that when it counted, she could be worth something.

That was why she was here. Ready to do what she had to, ready to face Zahir head-on, even while her knees shook slightly.

He looked at her, his dark eyes cold, disinterested. The flatness in them sent a chill straight into her soul, made her feel like she was staring into a bottomless, empty well. His face, distorted by injury, made him seem less human.

He inclined his head. "You are dismissed."

She looked at him, her mouth dropping open. "Excuse me?" She'd never been dismissed in her life.

"I have been trying to excuse you for the past ten minutes. Get out of my office."

"I will not," she said. Because she couldn't. But for one second she wished she could. Just for a moment. That she could walk out of his dark office and into the bright Hajari sunlight, head to the market, the mall and melt into the crowd.

Just for a second. And then she remembered. Remembered that she had to do this. Because if she didn't, Alexander would be shoved to one side while John claimed the throne, and if he managed to change laws to keep himself on there permanently...or even the possibility of him spending six years messing with the economy. It was unacceptable.

And it would mean she'd failed. Failed at the one thing her father felt she would be useful doing.

Zahir stood from his position at his desk. She stepped backward, the move instinctive, the action that prey would take when it knew it was eyed by a predator. He was big.

Much bigger than she remembered. Broad and toned, his tunic shirt clinging to the muscles on his chest.

"Haven't you gawked long enough? Why don't you go, sell the tale of your encounter with me to the highest bidder?"

"That isn't why I'm here."

"No, of course not, you just want to marry me. Live here, in the palace." He rounded the desk with long strides and his gait languid for two steps before she noticed a break in the rhythm, before she noticed the slight limp that accompanied his movements. He stopped in his tracks then, arms crossed over his broad chest. "With me. Because how could Princess Katharine Rauch, from her idyllic Alpine country ever resist such an opportunity? Do you imagine you'll be having grand, Arabian Night–themed balls? Is that it? I am not Malik."

"I know that," she said, her throat tightening. She was losing control, losing her footing. She couldn't lose. She had given her word to her father. And she had made a blood oath to her people from the moment of her birth. She was born a Rauch, she was meant to protect her country. And this was the only way she was allowed to do it.

That sense of duty was like a weight on her shoulders, her chest. Some days it made it hard to breathe. But it was a part of her, of who she was.

Katharine's heart rate kicked up when he took another step toward her, the light in his eyes dark, his black eyebrows locked together. "If you think it doesn't matter, the difference between Malik and myself, then you live in a foolish fantasy. The reality is this." He simply stood there and she knew he meant him. His scars. The scars he'd gotten in the same attack on the royal family that had seen Zahir's parents, and Malik, killed. Not just the royal family, but citizens who had come to watch the procession through the city.

All because of a power grab from a neighboring country. For money and land. What despicable things men did for both. She was trying to keep the same from happening in her own country.

His lip curled into a sneer, tugging at the scar tissue on his cheek. While part of his lip curled up, the edge of his mouth turned down slightly, fused there by a thick ridge of badly healed flesh. "Is this the man you want in your bed at night? For the rest of your life?"

Her eyes went then, not to his face, but to his hands. Large hands, wide and square, they bore scars too. But they also looked like they possessed strength, confidence. The images in her mind were quick and hot, dark hands on pale skin.

Katharine's body heated from the inside out, warmth pooling in her stomach and spreading slowly through her. The way that he said it was intended to sound like a threat, but his deep, smooth voice made it sound like a promise. Rather than repel her, it fascinated her on a level she didn't quite understand. No, he didn't frighten her, but that feeling did. Foreign and strong, filling her with adrenaline and languor at the same time, weakness and strength.

She didn't know how it had happened. How simple words had affected her like that. She threw it off, pushed ahead. She wasn't here to be intimidated; she was here to get what she needed. "There is an agreement."

"Out," he said, his voice hard, rough.

"I can't do that. I need to see that this marriage happens, for the good of both of our people. If you can't see it, I…"

He took another step toward her, so close now she could feel the heat radiating off his body. And not just heat. Rage. And for one fleeting moment a grief that she could almost feel echoing inside of her. It went beyond the strength of normal feelings, and she had the feeling that if it ever found its hold in her, in anyone, it would fill them completely. Consume them completely. It made her wonder how he was able to stand.

And yet he did. Strong and tall.

"I want to be left alone," he said, the words flat and cold, final in the stillness of the room.

She looked at him, at his face, at the exquisite bone structure beneath his damaged skin, high cheekbones, square jaw, straight, prominent nose. Smooth, olive skin was still present on one side of his face. Beautiful, compelling, offering a glimpse at the man he had been.

But there was nothing beautiful about the scars that marred the other half of his face. They were evil, ugly things that broadcast his pain to the world.

There was something about his eyes, though. They were still enticing, mesmerizing. Fringed with thick, dark lashes, the color of them so dark they seemed black. Even though it was clear one lacked sight, they were incredible eyes. Intelligent and piercing.

Most importantly, they reminded her that he was a man. Not a beast. She could see him in there this time, Zahir, as he had been before the attack. The man she had once met, so many years ago. She had barely spoken with him, but she remembered him. Always quieter than his brother, his face more serious, sort of aloof. All of him had been beautiful then. Captivating in a way that few people were.

He was still captivating, but it wasn't in the same way.

"This isn't about want, Zahir," she said, using his name to enforce the fact that he was only flesh and blood. Even if he was big, scary flesh and blood. "This is about doing what's right. It's about honor."

He looked at her a long time, his expression unreadable. And yet he was searching her, in her. She could feel it. "You assume, Princess, that I am in possession of honor."

"I know you are." It was more of a hope than a certainty, but it sounded good at least.

"Get out." He spoke the words softly, but the command was as powerful as if he had shouted it.

Failure was a foreign sensation to Katharine. She had never failed. She had spent all her life succeeding, proving that she was worthy of the sort of respect her brother had simply been born with. The highest test results, the most successful fundraisers. If a task was given to her, she completed it.

She hadn't accounted for what she might do if she failed here. As she'd boarded her family's private plane that morning she'd done so with confidence, enough that she'd sent both plane and pilot back to Austrich already.

In so many ways, failure was not an option.

"Fine," she said stiffly.

She turned and strode out of his office, her hands clenched tightly at her sides. He slammed the door behind her and she jumped.

Wretched man. Wretched, wicked, *beastly* man.

She hadn't counted on this. Obviously there was a possibility he would say no but…she was right. There was no question. She had thought he would see it. That he would understand what had to be done. Instead, he had…growled at her.

Katharine stood in the middle of the empty hall, arms crossed, trying desperately to hold in the body heat that was leaching from her in spite of the hot desert air. She didn't quite know what to do next. Where to go. Not home. She wouldn't be welcome anyway, not with the news of such a massive failure.

Footsteps echoed in the corridor behind her and Katharine turned. There was an older woman walking toward her. She recognized her. She'd been the *Sheikha's* personal servant, and had accompanied the S'ad al Din family to Austrich.

She searched her brain for a name. "Kahlah?"

The older woman turned and treated Katharine to a slight bow and a warm smile. There was no surprise visible in her lined face, but Katharine imagined she'd been trained to keep her emotions buried all of her life. She knew the feeling.

"Princess Katharine, it has been too long. Do you have business in Hajar?"

"I…" Technically speaking, she did, even though she'd already dealt with it, and been met with a resounding no. "Yes, I do."

Katharine's mind started working overtime. Zahir didn't want her here, that much was clear, but she needed to be here. Because she wasn't going home having failed her objective. That was an impossibility.

"I will be staying here at the palace for the duration of my time in Hajar."

"This is very welcome news, Princess Katharine. We have not had guests in… It has been a long time." That statement had brought a flicker of emotion to the older woman's eyes.

Katharine was certain there hadn't been guests since the attack. Everything in the palace was different than her last visit. Darker. Quieter. An echo with every footstep. It felt empty.

"Well, in that case I am honored to be the first guest in so long." She felt a slight prickle of guilt. But only a slight one. Zahir was being unreasonable and she needed time to come up with another angle. She just needed some time.

"Can you send some men out to the main entrance?" Katharine asked. "My driver is still there and my luggage is in the car. If you could have them install me in the same quarters I stayed in last time that would be satisfactory."

She put on her best regal princess voice. She was a terrible liar. Always had been. Her eyes gave her away. Fortunately Kahlah didn't seem to be paying attention to her eyes.

Kahlah looked unsure, but Katharine knew that the other woman wouldn't dare question her word, not in front of her.

Katharine felt like a first-class heel taking advantage of her as she was, but it was for the greater good.

*Certainly not for my good, which must mean I'm not being selfish at least.*

"Would you like me to direct you to your quarters, Princess?"

"If you wouldn't mind. But don't worry about my luggage. Have my things sent at the convenience of the staff. I don't wish to throw off anyone's schedules."

She'd brought enough clothing and essentials for an indefinite stay, because one thing she'd known for certain when she left home that morning: she was going to succeed. No matter what it took.

She was a princess who couldn't rule. One who had resigned herself to having little value beyond the light charity work she'd thrown herself into over the past couple of years. But this, this was big. This was her chance to change the course of things.

To be something more than beauty and a royal lineage.

"But of course, it is no trouble."

"I very much appreciate it." Katharine caught herself twisting the large sapphire ring on her right hand, nerves and guilt making her twitchy. She put her hands resolutely back at her sides. Princesses did not twitch.

Kahlah extended her arm. "This way, Princess."

Katharine walked next to Kahlah, looking everywhere but at the other woman. She busied herself with memorizing her surroundings, the route they were taking.

There was no matching the palace in the capital city of Kadim for opulence. Every surface made from glimmering marble, trimmed in brushed gold, the floor a glossy mosaic of jasper, jade and obsidian.

It didn't glitter in the same way it had five years ago. But it was still a testament of wealth and craftsmanship, the finest the country had to offer, she was certain.

A good thing. Because if the she was going to tempt the Beast of Hajar's wrath, she might as well do it while surrounded in luxury.

"What the hell is going on?" Zahir growled when he walked into the main area of the palace to discover a procession of suitcases being brought in.

There were trunks as tall as he was, large square cases and small leather bags.

The porter stopped in his tracks and looked in Zahir's direction, though not at him. They never did. "We're bringing in Princess Katharine's belongings, as directed, Sheikh Zahir."

"Directed by who?" he asked, ignoring the strange sort of cold feeling that accompanied a breach of his personal space. A loss of control.

The man edged away from Zahir, his nerves palpable. "By Princess Katharine."

Zahir didn't let the man finish his sentence before he turned and stormed out of the entry chamber and went toward the women's quarters. Of course, for all he knew she had gone and installed herself in *his* room.

In his bed.

His body tightened at the thought. A near alien sensation, one that was only half-remembered at this point in time. No, she wouldn't do that. Not even she was so bold. Or so perverse. As a woman would have to be to pursue a night in his bed.

He saw one of the maids slipping out of one of the bedchambers, closing the door behind her before she rushed off in the opposite direction, acting as though she hadn't seen him. She probably had. But even the staff tried to avoid him when possible.

He approached that door and pushed it open. And there she was, standing in the center of the room, her pale strawberry-gold hair loose around her shoulders now. Her simple blue dress, belted at the waist, was demure enough, and yet, the way it skimmed her lush curves easily set fire to a man's imagination.

Especially when that man's imagination had been left to dry up for so many years.

"What exactly are you doing here, *latifa*?" he asked, the word *beauty* escaping his lips before he had a chance to think better of it. Because, as simple as that, she was beauty. She embodied it. It was a shame that the desert withered beauty, the intensity too much for anything so delicate and soft.

She turned to look at him, green eyes icy. Perhaps she was not soft. Though she looked as though she would be to the touch. Her skin pale like cream, her curves lush.

His body stirred. His gut tightened. It had been a long time since a woman had affected his body like this. Since he had been affected in almost any way. Any way beyond the endless loop of torment that seemed to play on repeat inside of him.

"I'm staying," she said, her neck craned, her expression haughty.

"I told you to get out."

"Of your office."

"Of the country. And you knew what I meant."

She folded her arms. "I'm afraid that's not acceptable."

He moved to her and he saw her shrink slightly, her shoulders tucking in just a fraction. She wasn't immune to him, to his face, the ugliness that ravaged his looks, no matter how confident and unaffected she tried to pretend to be.

Her scent caught hold of him, light and flowery. Feminine. As he'd been reminded just a moment before, even the maids stayed far away from him. How long had it been since he'd been so close to a woman? It had been before everything, he was certain of that.

"What isn't acceptable is you parking your pretty royal ass where it's not welcome," he growled, using crude words to intimidate, since his looks alone hadn't done the job. Most people shrank away when they saw him, fear evident on their faces. Not Katharine.

She arched one pale eyebrow, her expression placid. "Compliments will not move me, I'm afraid."

Any fear and uncertainty she'd shown had been momentary, and now she met him face on, her gaze unflinching, her posture straight. He couldn't remember the last time that had happened, either. His staff avoided looking at him too closely if they could help it. And his people...they didn't seem interested in having him as a public figurehead. So long as he kept things moving.

His looks bolstered his reputation, or perhaps it was the other way around. Either way, rumors of their sheikh, scarred, possibly mad, kept the majority of them from wanting him to make public appearances. Those who did, who had attached some sort of idea of him being beyond mortal, a savior of some sort, they were the fools. And they were too afraid to approach him, too. Either one suited his purposes. It kept people out, and it allowed him to rule from within his palace.

It was not his people he set out to intimidate, but anyone who might try to attack them again. So far, it had worked.

But Katharine the Great didn't seem to care. She was all prickles, ice and confidence. Standing in his home as though it was her domain.

It was time to make the most of his beastly reputation.

"You want marriage, Katharine?" he asked, his voice a low growl. "You want to be my woman?" He drew closer to her, reached a hand out and ran his finger along one pale, petal-soft cheek. She was like silk. He wanted to touch more of her. All of her. He squashed the impulse. He had denied, no, he had been absent any of those desires for five years. It wouldn't hurt him to ignore them a while longer. "You want to warm my bed and have my children?"

Her face flushed scarlet. "No."

"I thought not."

"But I don't need to. Not for my purposes."

"You don't need heirs?"

She faced him with a hard stare. "Not from you. And if everything goes according to plan I won't need them at all."

He gritted his teeth, trying not to envision what creating heirs with her would entail. As he tried to keep his blood ice, keep the fire at bay. He had to keep hold of his control or… he didn't want to know what might happen. "Why is that?"

"Because, if my father dies before Alexander reaches legal age, I need you to be named Regent, not my cousin. I'm a woman, and I can't do it. I can't protect my brother. If John ends up on the throne…we're facing possible civil war, a hostile seizing of the throne. If it comes to war it's bound to affect your country, at least as far as trade is concerned."

"So what exactly are you proposing?"

"Whatever you want. I need this marriage, for my people. I will be your wife in your bed if you want, or your wife in name only. But the choice is up to you. If you refuse, the blood of my people is on both of our hands."

# CHAPTER TWO

BLOOD. Enough of it had already been spilled in the world. Enough of it seemed to stain him. It never seemed to come clean. No more. There could be no more.

"Explain," he said.

She took a breath, her breasts rising and falling with the action. "If my father dies before Alexander comes of age, a Regent must be put over him, ruling in his place until he is able to take the throne. If I am married, the position will go to my husband, if not, it goes to the nearest male relative. It so happens that if my closest male relative even gets the tiniest bit of power, I'm certain he'll do all he can to keep it. With him in charge at best we're looking at a total economic collapse, at worst, civil war as he attempts to make his position permanent. I will not stand by and watch that happen. Not while I have the power to change things."

Katharine's words carried fire, a passion that nothing in him could match. She didn't just care for her people, she took the mantle of leadership wholly and completely on herself. As Malik had done. She would have been well-suited to his brother. As always, thoughts of Malik, of his family, brought a heavy, oppressive weight to his chest. Reminded him that he wasn't the right man to stand here.

He wasn't made for massive parties, drafting laws and keeping the delicate balance between neighboring countries.

He was about action. Physical action. A joke now, as even that was limited, not just by his position, but by a body that, even after five years, didn't feel like it could possibly belong to him. It was like being locked in a prison cell. But there was no key, there wasn't even a door.

"Find someone else, Katharine. I'm sure there are all manner of titled men who would fight to the death over the *honor*. I, however, am not one of them."

"That isn't the point. The agreement is done, everything lined out, from the amount of power you will possess over Austrich to which of our children would inherit what, not that that will be a concern for us."

There was a moment, so brief he might have imagined it, that he saw vulnerability in her deep green eyes. And that brief moment nearly hit him. Nearly made him lose his grip on the internal shield he held so tight.

He tightened his jaw. "Your situation is regrettable…for you." He turned to go and he heard Katharine's high heels clicking, quick and sharp, against the hard floor.

"For both of us," she said. "If John takes control of my country he'll change everything. We have a good thing going between our two countries now. We're a huge buyer of your oil supply and you depend on us to supply produce, meat, wool. I don't see him keeping up with trade agreements. He's a blind, selfish fool. He'll be the downfall of Austrich and he'll do his best to shake Hajar with his incompetence as well."

He stopped and turned, his pulse pounding hard. One thing he had done as a leader was his absolute best to create a secure country for his people. To prevent the possibility of more attacks. Of more death. Katharine painted a bleak picture, one that made flashes of light go off in his mind.

Explosions and chaos. Confusion. Pain. Darkness.

He tightened his hand into a fist and squeezed. Hard. Working at bringing the walls back up.

He didn't want this to be his problem. He wanted to go on as he had, maintaining the balance, living alone. And yet he wasn't sure it could be ignored. A hot surge of adrenaline pumped through him, the automatic fighter's instincts filling him, fueling him. There had been a time when he'd been a warrior, when he'd been on the front lines.

He could picture what civil war would be like. He'd experienced a taste of that hell.

"In name only, and then what?" he asked.

"You can divorce me as soon as Alexander turns twenty-one."

"And what of your cousin then?"

"He's power mad, but he doesn't possess the wealth or connections to cause any trouble on his own. However, if he can get into power and start war…incite riots…he can declare a state of emergency and keep himself on the throne. That I can't have." She took a step toward him, extended her arm, her fingers hovering just above his forearm. She moved slightly, grazing him with her fingertips. "I will do whatever you ask of me."

He was hard as rock in an instant. His body's reaction nearly made him laugh. If she planned to use seduction to make her case then he would win, no question. She would never be able to bring herself to go through with it. And he would have the chance of watching her recoil in horror when she saw the extent of his injuries.

More than the injuries, it was the horror she would feel when she caught a glimpse of the man beneath the iron control. Hollowed out. Unfeeling. Left damaged and bleeding, wounds that would never heal into the blessed, hardened scars that had formed on the outside of his body. There was nothing whole left in him. All he had left was the will to go on, to rule his country, to do as his father would have wanted. As his brother would have done. Anything more was too much. Impossible.

Katharine braced herself. For him to yell. For him to do… something befitting a man with his reputation.

The idea of a temporary marriage had only just come into her mind, and now, she was desperate for him to take it. Because the idea of staying here, with him, for the rest of her life…she didn't think she could handle that. The palace felt abandoned, the staff at a minimum and Zahir…his disdain for her presence was palpable.

He almost made her long for her father's chilly presence.

And if she did marry him in name only, at the end, her job would be done. A feasible term instead of the life sentence she'd always imagined. A glimmer of hope she hadn't realized she'd wanted.

If she could change things…if she could give Alexander time to grow up then she and Zahir could divorce and everything would be set to move forward smoothly.

She could do something else. Be someone else.

Her pulse pounded in her temples. She hadn't really let herself hope for that outcome. That her marriage to Zahir really could be nothing more than paper. A paper easily destroyed later.

"A legal marriage only," he said, his voice hard.

"So much the better," she said, trying to keep the relief from showing through in her tone. "We can both go our separate ways later. And this way we preserve the peace between our nations." She started pacing, nervous energy demanding that she find a way to relieve it. "And when we do separate it will be amicable, naturally, so the link between Austrich and Hajar will remain strong."

Zahir turned his head slightly and she realized he was tracking her movements that way. She'd forgotten about his sight for a moment. Or at least the issue she'd assumed he had with his sight. She truly didn't know for sure.

"It must look real," he said.

She inclined her head. "Of course it must, if not like a love match, then like a permanent marriage. To my father, to John, to Alexander. None of them can know."

His upper lip curled slightly. "My people cannot know."

She realized then that it was a matter of his pride. She felt a slight pang in her chest. This would cost him, this man who lived in the shadows. But she couldn't even contemplate what the consequences would be if she didn't pull this off.

"No one," she said, her pledge to him.

"You will remain here."

"What?"

"What did you imagine would happen?"

"I had thought…my father is ill. I had thought to return home."

"Ah, and you do not think anyone will see that as strange? That my new wife has abandoned me?" He reached out and curled his fingers around her arm, just above her elbow, his black eyes burning into hers even as her flesh felt branded by his touch. "No one will know."

She explored his face visually for a moment. The ravaged skin, the slashing scar that interrupted the shape of his top lip. He could not be called handsome, not now. But he was compelling, fierce. And for a moment she was almost overcome by the desire to skim her fingers over his ruined cheek, to feel the damage for herself.

She clenched her hand into a fist and kept it glued to her side. "You have my word, Sheikh Zahir."

"As tradition dictates, you will stay here in the palace to cement the engagement," he said. She could tell that cost him. That he truly didn't want her here. She also knew that he wanted to keep up appearances.

She swallowed hard, feeling as though a judge had just lowered the gavel, sentencing her. *At least it's not a life sentence.*

"I will stay." It took every ounce of strength she had to speak, to not shrink away.

But she would use every shred of it that she had in her body to get through this. To see her country—her brother—through. To the other side. For freedom for her people. A new kind of freedom for herself. One where duty to the masses wasn't so much more important than living her own life.

It was a dream. And yet it was a dream that kept her going. That spurred her on now. She would rest later. She would have the chance to, something she'd not thought possible.

"I was planning on staying," she said. "For a while at least."

"I know, I saw your procession of belongings coming in earlier."

"It was too important. I wasn't going to back down."

"Why is it so important to you? Why are you the one who has to solve this? A matter of honor?" He regarded her closely, and she knew he truly wanted an answer.

"What would you do to ensure Malik's success, Zahir? If he lived, what would you do to make sure that he was able to fulfill his destiny? To make sure he was safe?"

His Adam's apple bobbed and she watched as his hands, both marred with scar tissue, flexed into fists. "Anything. I would give my life."

"As I'm giving mine."

He tilted his face up, angling the smooth side to her. "So noble of you." She was struck again by how beautiful he was in part. By how handsome he had been. The reminder was there. That square masculine jaw, perfect olive skin. There was no light in his eyes though, no emotion to read.

"I don't know about that."

"Modesty does not become the sort of woman who would storm the palace of Hajar and take up residence without permission," he said. And for a moment she thought she saw one side of his mouth curve upward. An expression of good humor. Although, that couldn't be. It really didn't seem possible.

"My apologies."

"One thing you must understand, *latifa*. The palace runs in a certain order, I do things on a certain schedule. You will not interrupt that."

No. Of course not. She wasn't important enough to interrupt the Almighty Schedule. Though, why that should bother her at all, she wasn't sure. Yes, she was. Common courtesy. She wouldn't say that to a regular palace guest, let alone one she was engaged to be married to. Even if it was going to be strictly a legal marriage.

"It's a big palace," she said. "I'll bet you can avoid me altogether if you like."

"A theory I am tempted to test."

"If we're going to pretend this is real you're going to have to work on treating me as though you want me around."

He leaned in and she pulled away slightly. His masculine scent teased her, made her heart accelerate. He had a scent all his own. Sandalwood and spice mingled with the musky, unique essence of Zahir. It made her head feel fuzzy.

"And you are going to have to pretend you aren't repulsed by me."

"I'm not," she said. It was the truth. He was scarred but all the nonsense about him being a beast, somehow something other than a man, that was just plain ridiculous. "I won't lie and say I'm completely comfortable with you, but by the time we have an engagement party…"

"There will be no engagement party." The light in his dark eyes was fierce, almost wild.

"There has to be," she said. "It is tradition for brides in Austrich to…"

"You are in Hajar now," he said, his voice hard, unyielding. "You have come into my country, and I am now your sheikh. You made this choice. Remember that." He turned and walked out of her chamber, slamming the door hard behind him.

And for the first time since her plane had touched down in Hajar, she truly felt like she was in over her head.

# CHAPTER THREE

KATHARINE finished pinning her hair in place and stared at her reflection. She was pale and red-eyed from lack of sleep. She looked like the walking dead. Very attractive. Fortunately her future husband didn't seem to care how attractive or unattractive she was. And she didn't care what he thought, either.

It was all about politics. All about what the union could bring both of them. Their countries.

She blew out a breath and turned away from the mirror, walking out of her room and into the vacant hallway. She wasn't going to stand around all day.

She should call her father. She'd picked up the phone about eight times since getting out of bed, but she just hadn't been able to bring herself to do it. Not yet. It would make it all too real.

How ironic that now she'd achieved her goal she was having trouble accepting it.

*It's nothing more than a ceremony and a piece of paper. At least you're not expected to stay with him forever, have his children.*

Now that would have been a harsh reality. One she'd thought she'd been prepared to deal with, but one she was certain now she hadn't been. Not if the thought of a marriage ceremony was affecting her this badly.

She headed down the long hall, the sound of her high heels

echoing off the high, domed ceiling. The corridors were extensive, weaving through the massive palace. But she knew where Malik's quarters had been, situated on the opposite end of the palace from where the women stayed. It was likely Zahir stayed in them now.

Yes, last night she'd spoken to him about avoidance. And then he'd tried to intimidate her by reminding her whose country she was in. But she wasn't easily intimidated. She'd spent her life surrounded by strong men, holding her own against a father who expected the worst and never praised her for her best. She always had to show strength.

She would never inherit the throne of Austrich. She was a woman, and for some reason, her lack of male member made her ineligible. But she was involved in the politics of her country, and she did not have a reputation as a shrinking violet. She didn't avoid conflict. She faced them head-on. And right now, she was looking for the tall, muscular conflict she'd tangled with the night before.

She looked into a couple of empty rooms before pushing open a door that revealed what could have been a modern, state-of-the-art gym. A lap pool, every sort of exercise equipment anyone could ever want.

And there was Zahir. Flat on his back on a weight bench, his breath hissing between his teeth as he pressed two massive dumbbells up over his chest.

She crossed the room tentatively, her mouth dropping open slightly at the sight of his body. Every muscle was chiseled, as though it were carved into rock, the only sign it could possibly be part of a real man, and not a statue, was the bunching and shifting that happened with each breath and movement.

Golden skin, some smooth and perfect, some ravaged by injuries, all of it fascinating. Unlike any man she'd ever seen.

She blinked and took a sharp breath. "Aren't you supposed to have a spotter or...something?"

He stopped midmotion and swung his legs over the side of the bench, sitting up quickly, his ab muscles putting on a show with the swift motion. "What are you doing here?"

"I came to find you."

"What made you think that would be well received?"

"I didn't really think it would be," she said, fighting to keep her eyes on his face. She traced the scars on his cheek with her eyes, hoping it would keep her mind off his naked chest. "It didn't really bother me."

The tendons in his neck stood out, a muscle in his jaw jumping. "It wouldn't."

Her eyes drifted lower. "No…I…well, that's not really the point…I…"

"Seen enough?" He voiced the question in a near growl.

Her eyes flew back to his face. His expression was cold. Closed. His lip curled into a sneer.

"Yes," she said, feeling heat creep into her face. It wasn't that she'd never ogled a man before. But they weren't usually this naked, and she'd never been caught. Or at least, the men in question had been too polite to say, because she was a princess after all. Zahir didn't seem to care.

He bent over and picked up a white T-shirt from the floor, his fingers trembling slightly as he held it out. And then her eyes were drawn to an intricate web of scar tissue, places where she knew he'd been hit with shrapnel, burned by fire, and her stomach tightened.

He pulled the shirt on and covered her guilty pleasure and the pain that was threatening to steal every last rational thought from her head.

"I thought you might show me around a little bit today," she said. She hadn't thought any such thing but now she had to say something because it was awkward.

"You thought wrong, *latifa*. I have work to do."

"What sort of work?"

"The kind rulers do—you must know something of that."

"Truly, not so much. The royal family makes appearances, and gives speeches." It was a lie. She did a lot. Organized charities, budgets, fundraisers, and yet, it was what he seemed to think of her.

"Ignorance isn't your color," he said.

"Got me there," she shot back.

"I thought I might."

"I think we need to go over the original agreement drawn up by our fathers and make any alterations we see fit," she said.

"Do you?"

"Better now than after the vows, don't you think?"

"Are you always like this?" he asked.

"Yes. I've been told I'm impossible to deal with. I'm okay with that, actually, because I usually get my way." In some circles anyway.

He made a sound, short and harsh, that might have been a laugh. "I imagine you have your ways of making sure your needs are met."

She frowned. "If you're implying what I think you were, don't. I don't use my body to get what I want. I use my mind. Or were you not aware that women were capable of that?"

"I wasn't making a commentary on women, only on you."

"Well, I don't like the commentary."

"I've been told I'm impossible to deal with," he said, repeating her earlier words back.

"I'm imagining that's very true."

"I always get my way," he said, turning away from her.

He was so broad. His shoulders, his back. All the better to carry the weight of the world on them. And he did. She sensed that. Mostly because she felt like she did, too, sometimes.

"I promise you can get back to the business of ignoring

me…after we go over the agreement. And after you give me a tour of the grounds because I'm tired of feeling like I'm lost."

He wanted her gone. That much was clear. But she was committed. To seeing this through, to doing the best she could.

To proving she could do this.

"I'll go shower and I'll meet you in my office." He strode across the gym, headed to the shower, she supposed. He would uncover that amazing body again. For a moment she let herself envision it. Just for a moment.

"I'll see you there," she said, hoping he didn't notice just how delayed her response was.

The woman didn't take hints well. When he walked into his office, she was there, perched in the chair adjacent to his desk, her posture perfect, her legs crossed at those dainty ankles of hers. She didn't wear nylons, though. Her legs were bare.

That stuck out to him. Mostly because it was rare for a woman in her position. But then, it was much hotter here than it was in Austrich. It could also account for what seemed to be a wardrobe entirely populated by brief, fitted dresses. All very modest in the technical sense, but showing just enough to light his imagination on fire.

It would almost have been better if she'd been dressed in something completely transparent. At least then the mysteries would be solved. If she was as pale and smooth all over as she looked, how full and round her breasts were without the aid of undergarments…important questions that were now overtaking his brain.

If he had known that all it would take was the presence of a woman to reawaken his hibernating sex drive he might have brought one in a long time ago.

*To what end? To treat her to a front row show of your inner demons? To watch her run away screaming?*

Like Amarah had done.

He couldn't even blame her. He might be edging into beast territory now, but then…just after the attack…he had been nothing short of a monster.

He pushed all thoughts of Katharine's body to the side and chose instead to embrace the extreme annoyance, the muscle-clenching tension that crowded in on him when she was around.

"Don't look at me like that," she said.

"Like what?" He rounded his desk and sat in the plush leather chair that was positioned behind it. It was too short for him. Made for another man. His brother. He had never replaced it.

"Like you're shocked to see me here. I said I'd meet you here to discuss the agreement, and I am. It's complicated stuff. With my father's history of health problems there has always been the chance that whoever I married would have to stand in as Regent until Alexander reaches age, and that was, of course, taken into account when Malik was selected to be my…"

"Let me see." He held out his hand, palm up, and she produced a folded stack of papers, placing them in his hand.

He skimmed the documents. Most of the information pertained to the marriage. Heirs. Alliances and trade agreements. Toward the end was the section talking about what might happen if the king died prior to his heir coming of age.

"The decision-making power is yours. I don't want it," he said. "Write that in." He pointed to the spot.

She blinked rapidly, looking a bit like a stunned owl for a moment before shaking her head and leaning forward in her chair. "I can't. Not without bringing it to parliament. And I would need my father's permission and I…I don't think you'll get it."

"Is he too ill to hold a pen?"

Color crept up her neck, into her cheeks. "He would rather have the power rest with you."

"He doesn't trust you?"

She sucked in a breath, her hands clenched tightly in her lap. "Well, I'm a woman."

"I fail to see why that should matter. You have more guts than most men I've met."

Her lips curved slightly and a strange, heated sensation, almost like satisfaction, spread through his chest. It was warm, almost too much after so many years of experiencing nothing more than bitter cold.

She almost made him want to feel. Made him want to let go.

"He's a product of a different generation," she said. "I don't hold it against him." And yet he could tell she did. That it lived in her, drove her forward. He knew about things like that. All too well. "This is my responsibility as far as he's concerned. Protect the country by marrying a man capable of serving as Regent."

He looked at her face, so earnest, so determined. So beautiful. His pulse sped up, the heat spreading through him. "I have my own country to run, I would be absentee at best, negligent at worst."

"You couldn't be as negligent as my cousin would be in your sleep."

"Austrich will be your responsibility, whether we write it in the paperwork or not."

"I...thank you." She looked down at her hands, feigning an interest in her fingernails. "We have a parliament in place. It isn't as though I can change laws or budgets or anything like that. It's not terribly involved. Stand on the balcony and wave to the crowd."

The crowd.

He closed his eyes and braced himself, a sharp flash, hazy,

fast-moving images assaulting his mind as reality, his office, the desk, broke away piece by piece to make room for the memories. The crowd. Thick and loud. Surrounding the motorcade. It took a moment to realize that the barricade had been broken. That the people surrounding them weren't citizens offering their greetings to the royal family.

It was all he could see. The sound deafening, roaring in his ears. The smell of smoke and sulfur filling his nose, the smoke choking him, his lungs burning. He couldn't breathe, couldn't think.

"Zahir?" Her voice broke through the fog.

He opened his eyes again and saw only his office. And Katharine, sitting there, looking at him. He could see concern in her clear green eyes. She had noticed. What had he done? He realized then that his fist was clenched tight, resting on the desk, so tight that his tendons were screaming at him.

He had lost himself for a moment. Lost where he was.

It didn't happen as often now as it had. Because he knew better than to let his guard down now. Than to let emotion take over control. She had distracted him. And now she'd seen him... She had seen his weakness.

"I don't do that," he said, his throat constricted. *Dammit.* "The crowd thing, I mean." He took a breath and tried to re-orient himself. "I have more of a face for radio."

She smiled again, this time the expression was tinged with a bit of discomfort, as if she wasn't certain what the appropriate response was.

"You can laugh, it's okay," he grated.

She did then, a soft laugh, but it brought that feeling back, the warm one, stronger, spreading. He stopped it this time, cutting it off with the force of a tourniquet on a wound.

"Well, I make a lot of appearances," she said.

"I know. You always seem to be in the news. Your fashion sense is much written about."

She nodded. "Of course. Although, I often wonder if anyone would care what color tie I wore if I was a man, but I can't really complain. It's nice to have my country featured in international news. Even if it is just for my shoes. It boosts tourism."

"Do you have a lot of tourism in Austrich?" He reached deep for control, for total control, to find that kind of blessed numbness he was so accustomed to.

"Only recently. But that's been part of what I've been involved with over the past five years."

Since his brother's death. She needed to stay busy, he supposed. If everything had gone according to plan, she would have married Malik on her twenty-first birthday.

She seemed to miss his train of thought, because she breezed on. "We have a tram system that takes people up into the Alps. You can't beat the views. And then there's various resort properties I personally have funded the development of. We were in need of luxury vacation spots, and now, Austrich has become a very popular spot for vacationing royalty."

"And that is partly due to your personal campaigning, I would think."

"Do you think I go to all those parties for the canapés?" She arched her brow.

"I did. But I would not think so now."

Katharine swallowed, hard to do around the sudden lump in her throat. Zahir, who wanted her here about as much as he might want a root canal, had just had a longer conversation with her about what she did than anyone in her family ever had.

Not only that, he seemed to understand. To see her as more than just a peripheral. Oh, her father was counting on her, he'd made that very clear. But he was counting on her to marry someone. Not to do anything that required her specifically. This had nothing to do with her skills or talents.

*You're beautiful. Of course he will say yes.*

Oh, yes, she was beautiful. Her father had been confident in that being her ticket to marriage with Zahir. Funny, but Zahir didn't seem to care at all. And if she didn't possess anything more than a pretty face she would have failed.

Something her father would probably never know. She loved him, she truly did, but he saw so little of her it was stunning at times. Heartbreaking at others. But she didn't have any energy to waste on feeling sorry for herself. Dealing with Zahir took everything she had.

"You might be surprised that some people *do* invite me to parties, though. Seeing as you've spent the better part of two days hoping to evict me."

"I have agreed to this now, Katharine, I will not back out. You have my word. My protection, as does your country. I don't give any of those things lightly." His hand tightened into a fist and she wondered if he was going to pound it on the desk again, as he had done a few minutes earlier. It had been so strange, as though he wasn't looking at her anymore. Like he was seeing something else. And then he'd been back, she'd seen the change in him.

It had scared her a little. Not for herself, but for him.

"This agreement," he said, "it is what my father saw as the right thing for Hajar. What Malik saw as right. Who am I to disagree?"

"Then I suppose it's time for me to call my family with the good news."

Zahir looked at her for a moment, those searing, dark eyes boring into her. "Why exactly are you doing this, Katharine? For honor? Truly and simply for the good of your people?"

"Yes," she said. She thought for a moment about whether or not this was the place to speak words she'd never dare say out loud before. But why not? In this room she'd given him honesty, and he had listened. He hadn't pretended there was no way she could have accomplished what she had.

"For that, and because it's the light at the end of the tunnel." She couldn't believe for a moment she'd truly said it. Because it was something she'd hardly acknowledged to herself. She'd been too afraid to. Afraid that if she admitted she was becoming unhappy with a purely duty-filled life she would find herself unable to complete the tasks set before her.

"In what way?"

"After our marriage ends…Alexander will be king. And I'll be…I will always feel responsibility for my people, loyalty to my family. I will always work for the improvement of my country, but… It won't have to be my sole focus anymore." Maybe then she would be free of that feeling. That gnawing sensation that no matter what she did, she wasn't doing enough.

He only looked at her, his expression unreadable.

"What about you?" she asked. "Do you have a light you're aiming for?"

His hands curled into fists again and his gaze shifted slightly, his throat working. "I'm glad you see a light, Katharine. For me, there is only darkness." He looked down then, shifted his focus to the computer screen that sat on his desk. "Now that we have all that settled, I have work do to."

# CHAPTER FOUR

KATHARINE hated being at a loose end. She never was back in Austrich. Her days were packed from start to finish. She reviewed their budget for charitable contributions, went to committee meetings and spent time volunteering at the largest hospital in the country. She never had a moment of her own, and that was fine with her. It made her feel...it made her feel useful.

But in Hajar there was nothing to do. No, specifically, in the palace there was nothing to do. She could only read for so long during the day before her eyes felt scratchy, and it was too hot in the middle of the day to do anything in the garden. She'd been out earlier, cutting flowers to add to the vacant vases she'd noticed when she'd first arrived. But the weather had moved past the point of sweltering, so now she was wandering the halls, staying cool thanks to the thick stone walls and that lovely air-conditioning they'd put in when they'd brought the palace out of the dark ages.

She was used to much cooler weather, crisp mountain air, not air that burned your lungs like fire when you sucked in a breath. Another part of the arrangement she hadn't calculated. Not back when she'd been intending to marry Malik in the true sense of the word, and not when she'd come and proposed to Zahir.

Everything was so different. And *she* was starting to feel different.

A loud curse and shattering porcelain broke the lull of boredom she'd fallen into.

She quickened her pace, weaving through the labyrinthine halls until she saw Zahir, standing in front of the massive stone table that was placed against the wall there, the antique vase she'd place flowers in earlier shattered into uncountable, unfixable pieces. The flowers didn't look like they'd survived the attack.

He looked up, his eyes black with rage. "Did you do this?"

"Did I do what? Maul those flowers?"

"Did you put the flowers here?"

"Yes, I put them in three vases that were empty. Here, in my room and in the entryway. Is that a dungeon offense these days?"

He walked over the ruined vase, his hard soled shoes grinding the shards of ceramic into powder, his gait uneven, the slight limp more pronounced than normal. "Do not change things like that without my permission." He spoke slowly, his voice low, deadly. "You had no right to do this."

A trickle of fear dripped through her, followed by a flood of anger that washed it away with its hot, fast tide. She stood, hands planted on her hips. "Don't be such a…"

"Beast?" he growled.

"I was going to say bastard, but whatever works best for you. You might not mind living in that dark, sparse palace but I do. And it's my home now, per your royal command, and it's going to be my home until the end of our arrangement. I am not asking your permission to make changes in my own home."

"It is not your home, *latifa*, make no mistake."

"Is this some kind of stupid testosterone thing? Have I impinged on your territory there, lone wolf?" Anger was

controlling her now, making her reckless, making her heart
pound hard.

"Do not mock me."

"Then don't behave in a way that's so…mockable."

"You don't understand. If you move things…"

"I didn't move anything I…"

"You moved this." He slammed his hand, palm down, onto
the stone table.

"And?"

"And I ran into the damn thing!" he roared.

His words echoed in the corridor, hanging there between
them, the reality slowly sinking into her mind. It stopped any
response she might have had cold in her throat.

He lifted his hand from the table and she noticed, for the
first time, that his palm was bleeding. Both of his palms
were bleeding.

"What…?"

"Stay back."

"Zahir…"

He swallowed. "I know where things are in my home. I
should not have to worry about anything being misplaced."

She felt dizzy, mortified. A heavy weight crushed her
chest. She had moved the table out from the wall, maybe
two inches, so that the blossoms wouldn't be squished. Such
a stupid, shortsighted thing.

Now it made sense. Now she could picture it. Him coming
out of his room, turning left. It would have been in the line
of his blind eye, where he could not see. And he would have
no reason to think anything had changed.

"I'm sorry," she said, her voice muted. "Your hands…"
She almost choked. He had fallen into the glass after knocking the vase over. What if he had hit his head? All because
she'd wanted to add flowers to the room.

"Don't move things," he said again, a tremor running

through his rough voice as he stood looking at her, black eyes fierce, his chest rising and falling sharply.

She tried to speak again, to say more impotent words of apology, but he turned and left her there, alone in the hall, pain spreading through her chest.

Not exactly a stellar way to start the day.

The best thing to do would probably be going after him But she didn't want to. She wanted to curl up in a ball and hide from her own uselessness. From the whole situation. She hadn't ever resorted to that tactic before, and she wasn't going to do it now.

On a shaky breath, she bent down, careful to avoid the glass, and gathered the flowers back up. She felt sick, defeated. Like the kind of idiot woman her father imagined her to be. Although, failing at household tasks like decorating might make her even lower on his personal totem pole.

For one, terrifying moment, she believed it. She believed she couldn't really do anything right. That she couldn't do this.

*No. You have to. You will do this.*

Her own personal pity party wasn't the important thing here anyway. What did matter was what that had cost Zahir.

"I'm sorry," she said to the empty space, her throat tightening over the words.

He didn't want to hear it from her, she knew that. He walked with a slight limp, one he did his best to mask, but she had noticed it. And she knew that something like this, something that forced him to acknowledge a weakness, a limitation, was the worst of nightmares. It was his pride that had suffered worst of all.

She just knew it, deep in her bones, as sure as she knew anything about herself.

She'd caused a problem, made a mistake, and now she was going to fix it.

* * *

Zahir took his fury, his humiliation, out on the pool in his gym. At least in the water his movements were smooth. He knew the length, knew just how many strokes it took to get to the end. Here there was no limp, his sight didn't matter.

He stopped and gripped the edge of the pool cursing loudly, dragging his hand and droplets of water down his face, his palm burning where his flesh had been left raw and cut by the broken vase. But he welcomed that pain. Physical pain meant little to him. He'd survived more of it than any man should be able to.

But making such a fool of himself, showing such weakness, that was a true blow. He never did that. Now he had done it twice with her.

He looked up and saw pale, delicate ankles, then up farther to a set of shapely legs. Had she been any closer to the edge of the pool, he would have been treated to a lot more.

The woman had no sense of boundaries. "What is it you want, *latifa*?"

He tightened his jaw, grinding his teeth. His towel was across the gym, and she was there, standing, staring. Another chance to shock herself with his ravaged body? She hadn't run the first time, but he did not go out of his way to show the scars that marred his body. Not out of vanity. But because they shamed him. Reminded him, every day, in every way, that he was less than he had been. That he shouldn't be here.

Survivor's guilt, his first doctor had called it. Naming it didn't change anything. How else was he supposed to feel? Should he forget? Move on from the event that had taken everyone? If he forgot, who would remember? Who would carry it with them? He felt as though he was keeping them here. Anchoring them to this world.

Impossible, he knew. And yet the feelings remained.

"What does that mean?" she asked.

He placed his palms flat on the rough cement surrounding the pool, welcoming the pain it brought, the distraction, as he hauled himself out of the water in one fluid motion, bracing himself for the less than agile feeling that came with having his own two feet beneath him. Putting weight on legs that didn't feel like they belonged to him.

Her eyes were glued to his torso and he fought the urge to cover himself. A strange, weak response. It should not concern him, what she thought of his body, of the scars that marked his skin, the deep groove that showed the loss of muscle and strength in his thigh.

He simply stood for a moment, daring her to look away. She didn't. But then, she never did anything he expected—why should she start now? He would almost be disappointed if she descended into predictability. Almost.

He reached over to the nearby towel rack to pull off a black towel, dragging it over his chest, then around to his back. She watched him the whole time, and he felt his body responding to the open, female appraisal. It had been so long since he had felt a woman's hands on his skin, and just as long since one had looked at him as though he were a man.

No one, other than his physician, had ever seen his body uncovered since the wounds had healed. Amarah had seen him when they were fresh. When there had been a hope of healing. They had been too much for her to handle then. Or, perhaps she could have handled the scars if the attack had only stolen his physical attraction. If it had not taken the very soul of who he was. Good that she'd run early so he hadn't had the chance to bring her down with him.

Of course, unlike his ex, Katharine wouldn't be running.

"It means *beauty*," he said, discarding the towel, crossing his arms over his chest.

She looked slightly surprised to hear the translation. "Oh. Well, I thought it might mean 'pain in the rear' or something."

A sharp twinge of amusement forced a laugh to climb his throat. "Not quite."

Full, pink lips curved into a smile and cut through the defense he'd put up between them. She appealed to his body, as a woman did to a man. A whole man. And for a brief moment, he felt as though he were.

It only took a sharp, shooting pain from his diminished thigh muscle to remind him that wasn't the case. Just like the desert would wilt a rose, he would wither Katharine, would steal the life from her.

Her pretty face contorted. "Oh, no, that's from the table, isn't it?"

He jerked his head back. "What?"

"The bruise on your leg and…" She moved toward him and he took a step away. "Your hands."

"What?"

She moved forward another step. "Let me see them." She reached out and took one of his hands in hers, palm up, examining the torn skin, moving the tip of her finger around one of his injuries. "Painful?" She was so soft. So warm. Alive.

It made him want to ask why she was touching a dead man. A man who was dead in all the ways that counted.

"Not in the least." He pulled his hand back, the burn of her touch lingering. "I have endured worse. This is nothing."

"It wasn't nothing earlier."

"I was angry."

"I know. At me. And my flowers had to die a horrible death because of it. Not that I really blame you. I didn't think, and I'm…I'm very, very sorry."

He held his hand up. "This? This will heal." Unlike the rest of him. That was the unspoken portion of that statement, hanging in the air between them.

He stood before her now, defiant, daring her to look away,

she was certain. But she couldn't. He held her captive. He turned away first. "What is it you want?"

"I have...I want you to have dinner with me." For the first time, she faltered, showed a hint of true nerves and vulnerability. His first instinct, one so long suppressed, was to reassure. And yet he couldn't figure out a way to do it, couldn't find it in him.

She pressed on. "I had your chef prepare some of your favorite foods. And some of mine. I thought we might...get to know each other a bit better."

The last thing he wanted. He needed her life and his life to remain separate, for his routine to be uninterrupted. He needed to keep his control, his order. He didn't need her making him want to...comfort. Because when the heat spread through him, his control slipped. And when his control slipped...

"How much money will be saved annually by the trade agreements our marriage will enact?"

Confusion flashed through her eyes. And he felt nothing. He embraced that. Embraced the void and the security it offered.

"Ten billion, conservatively."

He chose his next words carefully, designed to keep distance. Designed to make her as disgusted with him as she should have been from the start. "That is all I need to know about you."

She looked at him for a moment, eyes glittering, a determined set to her jaw, arms crossed beneath full breasts. "I'll be there. In the dining hall in half an hour."

Zahir cursed himself as he buttoned his shirt midstride, making his way through the maze of corridors toward the dining hall. What had happened to routine? And distance?

He cursed again.

He rarely ate in the formal dining area. Only if he was forced to entertain visiting dignitaries. Even then, he tried to send his advisor in his place. He wasn't the best face to put forward for Hajar. Most of his people—at least those in control of the media—would attest to that. He was no diplomat, no master of fine negotiations. He was a strategist, a planner. He had built up his nation's economy from behind the doors of his father's office. But when it came to physical meetings…

He was not the man to handle things in person.

He only had to think of Katharine's face when he'd slammed his bloody palm down on the table to drive that point home. He had frightened her. And he cared. He had no idea why he cared. Or why the image of her sitting at the table alone in that knee-length, red silk dress she'd been wearing made him feel…anything.

And yet it did. And he could not afford it. He knew it, knew the cost of a weak moment. A weak moment, a lax moment, could mean the difference between life and death. It had for his family. And now…a weak moment could mean the loss of his control.

Still he had come.

He walked through the arched doorway into the ornate dining area. The table was low with cushions lining it on all sides. Katharine was there, at the head of the table, naturally, her pale legs curled beneath her, her expression neutral. Her plate was empty, despite the fact that there was an abundance of food laid out on the table.

He knelt at the other end. "Sorry I'm late."

"No, you're not. You're late on purpose."

"No. I'm here on accident," he said.

She laughed, an annoyed laugh, if there was such a thing. "What does that mean?"

"That I wasn't going to come."

"I see." She stood up and took her plate with her, walking

slowly down the side of the table until she was right in front of him, the view of her legs from his position on the cushions an intoxicating and unexpected sight. She was close enough that he could reach out and touch her. Feel if those long legs were as soft as he imagined.

He had a brief flash, an image in his mind and he braced himself for the inevitable. But it wasn't a picture of chaos and violence. It was him, curling his fingers around her calf, pressing a kiss to her thigh, running the tip of his tongue up along her skin until…

He clenched his teeth together, fighting to keep himself, his body, on its tight, self-imposed leash.

She sat next to him, her arm brushing his, and his fantasy was disturbed.

"I'm not sitting across the room from you."

"Why not? Most people would." He picked a tray up from the table and put some figs, meat and cheese on Katharine's plate before serving himself.

"I'm not most people."

"Yes, I'm aware of that."

She always met his eyes. Always looked straight at him. No one did that. Not even staff who had been here before the attack. Though there were few of those left. It had been too hard for them to stay. Too frightening. Always wondering if the same people responsible for killing his family would come for Zahir. If they would be caught in the cross fire.

Amarah hadn't been able to look at him. She had tried. She'd worn his ring, was meant to be his wife, had professed to love him. And she had tried to take on the responsibility of caring for him.

He'd been half out of his mind then. Not wholly in the past or present. Not certain of what had happened. Sometimes sickeningly certain of what had happened, everything playing in his mind with horrifying clarity. From beginning to end, like a film he couldn't stop.

Even now, he only kept it all down with years of practice. Of keeping total, full control over his mind at all times.

Amarah hadn't been able to endure it. Had not been able to handle the changes that had happened in him. If the woman he loved, the woman who loved him, couldn't stay…couldn't face him…it was no surprise when no one else could, either. He was glad, in a way, that no one had ever tried. There was no point bringing them into his personal hell.

"This is my favorite," she said, reaching past him and picking up a platter. "Obviously it's not like my mother made it for me, but our chef did. Wild rice with pecans. Not a state dinner type of thing but…sort of comfort food for me."

"I'll try it." He lifted his plate and she served him a portion.

He wasn't certain he'd ever eaten this way before. It was strangely intimate, serving her, having her serve him. His family had been formal. Distant in many ways. And yet their absence was profound.

"I don't suppose your mother did the cooking, either?"

The thought of his mother, always so beautiful and serene in her long, jeweled robes, her black hair pinned up in an ornate style, made his chest feel tight. "No. She was good at delegating, though."

Katharine laughed, happier this time, a sound that worked to loosen the knot inside him. "Oh, me, too. Notice I didn't claim to cook any of this." She paused then tilted her head to the side, a shimmering, red-gold wave cascading over her shoulder. "Maybe I will cook someday."

"Once you reach the light at the end of your tunnel?"

"Yes. Maybe then. I'm going to move out of the palace. Traditionally, an unmarried princess would continue to live there, under the protection of her family, but I suppose a divorcée might do what she wants."

"You suppose?"

"No one in my family has ever divorced."

"No one?"

She shook her head, her strawberry waves catching the light. "No. I will be unique."

"I'm certain you already are."

"Perhaps too much, to the despair of my father."

"And you aren't concerned how that will be received?"

"My mother died when I was ten. My father will be gone soon…" Her voice was thick with sadness. "Only Alexander will be left and he won't care what I do. You know how younger brothers are."

He did. He had been one. Looking on Malik with nothing but respect. Never once had he envied him his position. Never once had he wanted to be him. And now look at him. He had stepped into his brother's life. He was even marrying his brother's intended bride.

The thought was like burning steel in flesh. Nothing fit in this life. Nothing was his. A constant reminder that the wrong man had lived through the attack on his family. It should have been Malik sitting here with Katharine. Ruling the country as their birth order dictated.

"I do."

"So, he'll accept what I'm doing with my life and be… happy for me, I suppose."

"Have you always resented your duty?"

She sat still then, the only motion the fluttering of her pulse at the hollow of her throat. "I have always accepted that I would marry someone for the sake of my country. When I met Malik…I felt good about what I was doing. It felt right. He was a good man and the alliance between the countries would provide so much protection for both of our nations."

"And when he died?"

"My heart felt torn in two."

Katharine looked down at her hands. It was the truth. The day she'd found out about the attacks, she'd felt that it had happened to her own family. She'd grieved the loss of the S'ad al Dins. Had grieved for the country, for the one who was left.

She hadn't loved Malik, but that didn't mean his death was painless for her. He had been a good man, one she'd been confident would do the best by his country and hers.

It had been devastating to lose that. And she'd felt aimless. Like she'd been searching for new purpose. Because she'd known, from day one, that it had been her duty to marry advantageously for Austrich.

With that gone, she'd had to find something new.

She had. The past five years she'd had more freedom, more aim than ever before. She'd made changes, had made valuable friendships. Had worked at proving herself in a way that went beyond her worth as breeding stock.

Coming back to the marriage part, that had been jarring. But again, she knew her place. But now…now that she'd tasted something else, something that was hers…it made her want more. It made her want to find out if she might find some contentment there.

"I did not know you felt so strongly for him," Zahir said, his words stiff, his dark eyes closed off.

"I felt very strongly about the arrangement. That's one reason I fought so hard for it. It's the right thing."

"And yet…since I will give you an out, you're more than willing to take it."

Shame made her face hot. "Yes," she said, the words a whisper.

"What's changed?"

"The thought that maybe I could have something else. Something more."

A muscle in his jaw ticked. "And in the meantime, you make yourself a human sacrifice."

"Haven't we both?"

"True. I know why you do what you do. Do you know why I am the Sheikh of Hajar? Why I didn't pass it to one of my distant relatives?" His voice was rough, his words halting. "Because I am the only one left to fight. And even if I have to fight for my people from a desk, I will do it until there is no more breath in me. Because I'm all that's left."

Her heart seized in her chest, the aching, emptiness of his loneliness swept through her, left her breathless. The move to touch him was reflexive, an instinct she couldn't fight. She covered his hand with hers and his body jerked, but his hand remained there, beneath hers.

He didn't speak, he only looked at her. But the look in his eyes became more focused as he did. His gaze drifted down to where her hand covered his, so pale next to the deep golden tone of his skin.

"I am sorry about before," she said, her voice a whisper.

He was silent for a moment, his hand tense beneath hers. "As am I."

She slid her hand away from his, but she felt the lingering heat from him. From his skin. "I spoke to my father and brother today."

"And?"

"My father is thrilled, of course, well, in his way, and… Alexander doesn't really know the circumstances. I don't want him to. He'd hate to know that I was doing this for him. He's only sixteen and he simply wouldn't understand. And neither of them know that this is…temporary."

"I see. When did you understand you were to marry a man your father selected?"

She laughed softly. The memory of that day was one she tried her best to block out on most occasions. "Maybe twelve. It came up at dinner. My mother had passed away just a couple of years earlier and Alexander was just a toddler. My father mentioned that he'd begun looking for…I think he used the words *appropriate suitors* for me. I was appalled."

"I would imagine so."

"I had posters of my favorite singer on my wall and I was going to marry him. Somehow I didn't think a pop star would pass muster."

She was gratified when his lips turned up into a slight smile. "I would think not."

"What about you?"

"Malik was the one who had to think about advantageous marriages."

"Yes, that was meant to be me."

He looked at his wineglass. "I was going to marry for love."

Her stomach tightened. Before the attack, he meant. "You still can. After."

He shook his head. "I think not. I don't believe in it anymore. And even if I did, I know I can no longer feel it." He pushed up on the edge of the table, his movements jerky. "Thank you for dinner."

"Thank the chef," she said, trying to suppress the sadness that was mounting in her.

"I will." He inclined his head and turned away from her, leaving her sitting at the table alone.

# CHAPTER FIVE

KATHARINE had been in Hajar for more than a week and the walls of the palace were starting to crush her from the inside out. She was feeling a definite need to get out and see more of the country, or at least see more than the inside of the palace, beautiful though it was.

She'd heard they had some magnificent upscale shopping centers in Kadim, the capital city, but she'd yet to see anything beyond the airport and Zahir's home.

At least now she was on her way out. She'd spoken to Kahlah that morning about obtaining security detail for a shopping excursion and her needs had been met quickly. Now, just an hour later, she was headed into the city.

She hadn't spoken to Zahir, but he hadn't been in his office or the gym, and it wasn't as though he'd given her a way to contact him. She was beginning to wonder if he ever left the palace.

A sickening weight settled in her stomach. He was like a prisoner in some ways, and yet, he was the one who'd sentenced himself. But she could sense it. Could sense that there was a dark energy in him that was boiling beneath the surface. And that he held it back, along with so many other things.

She could see the skyline of the metropolitan city beyond the highway, providing an elegant and unexpected backdrop to Old Kadim, which was still prominently in the foreground.

The buildings made of stone, the narrow roadways lined with open-air markets.

There was a flavor to it, unexpected so near the modern, gleaming brilliance of the city beyond. It fascinated Katharine. Called to her.

As the car passed one of the markets, Katharine craned her neck to see. It was crowded, people out doing daily errands, and tourists who were enjoying the Old World atmosphere of the open-air shopping.

"I'd like to stop here for a while, if that's all right."

The two men in front exchanged glances, then nodded and the driver pulled the car into the nearest parking spot—a spot Katharine was a bit skeptical was in fact designed for parking, but that seemed to be driving in Hajar. People following their own arbitrary rules.

The security team got out before her, in a move that seemed a touch obvious, then came and opened her door. "Thank you," she said.

The men were glued to her side as she made her way from the car down into the main hub of the market. "You can walk behind me," she said. "Just a little bit."

When she went shopping in Europe she always had security with her, but they weren't usually so big. Or hulking. Or obvious.

She breathed in, the sharp scent of meat, spice and dust mingling together, tickling her throat. It was loud here. Talking, laughing and music melting together, indistinguishable from each other.

"I'm going this way," she said to her detail.

They followed silently, their expressions stoic, their manner no less obvious than it had been a moment earlier.

The crowd was thick and people rushed past her, some nearly running into her. Strange to think that this would be her home for the next few years. It was so different to anything she was used to.

She watched as a mother bent down and picked a screaming child up from the ground. So different, but the same, too. She smiled and turned to one of the stalls, touching one of the glittering necklaces that was tacked onto a flat of velvet with a small nail.

"What is this?" Zahir's voice, hard, angry, cut through the noise of the market like a knife.

She released her hold on the necklace. "This is me…shopping. How did you know where I was?"

"Kahlah. I certainly didn't hear it from you. Why didn't you tell me where you were going?"

People were pausing to stare. Truly, they were gaping openmouthed at Zahir. From what she knew of him, he never made public appearances. He had a face for radio he'd said, and he addressed his people that way. There had also been very few pictures taken of him since the attack, none close up.

But they knew who he was. And it was clear that some were awed, others horrified. Frightened. Because so many of them believed him to be a devil. A beast. Zahir didn't seem to notice at all. His eyes were on her, and her alone.

He closed in on her and took her arm. "This isn't safe."

"I have security with me."

"I had security," he roared. "We all had security. It didn't do any good."

"Zahir…"

His hand tensed around her arm as more people began to crowd around them, people who had walked through her as though she was invisible. Not now. Add Zahir to the equation and everyone was riveted to the drama unfolding.

He paused for a moment, his body stiff. She saw the same strange, distant look in his eyes, as though he wasn't seeing her, as though he wasn't seeing what was around. His eyes locked with hers, bottomless wells of dark emotion. He was like a hunted animal, all fear and rage and primal instinct.

That was when she knew he saw her, unlike the time in his office. But there was something wrong. He wasn't in this moment. He was in another time, gripped with an emotion so strong that it had dragged him down into the depths of it.

He pulled her away with him, out of the crowd, to one of the crumbling brick buildings behind a market stall. She stumbled, and he held her steady, his strength enhanced by the adrenaline she knew was screaming through him.

They rounded a corner, slipping into a narrow alleyway, and he pressed her against the wall of one of the surrounding buildings, his big body acting as a shield. From what, she didn't know. His hands were pressed flat against the brick on either side of her, his chest against hers. He was hunched over her, the gesture protective, feral.

His breathing was harsh, unsteady, each gust of air bringing a near growl with it that seemed to rumble through his being. His entire body was rock hard with tension, every muscle, every tendon straining as he fought to keep himself strong against her.

"Zahir," she said, her voice soft.

He didn't move, he only stood, braced, a human barrier between her and whatever danger he thought they faced. She lifted her hand and put it on his chest, felt his heart beating hard against her palm. She felt his pain. His fear. It was in her, squeezing around her heart, suffocating. Horrendous.

And she could only imagine what it was to be in Zahir's body now.

She slid her hand up, her fingers curling around his neck. He lifted his head, his dark eyes blazing with something wild, intense. She moved her hand upward, resting it lightly on his cheek, his skin rough beneath her fingertips. "Everything's fine. We're just in the market."

He shuddered beneath her touch, his eyes closing for a long moment before he opened them again.

She lifted her other hand, resting it on the smooth side of his face, and looked into his eyes. "Zahir."

He swallowed hard, and she felt him shiver, the muscles in his body spasming. "Katharine."

He pulled away from her. Katharine was relieved to see that the crowd had dispersed, thanks in part of Taj and Ahmed and their ham-handed style of security, she imagined.

"I'm fine," she said.

"Get in the car," he said tightly.

She nodded once, moving ahead of him. She kept her head down, ignoring the stares and the conversation in languages she didn't understand.

"No," he said. "My car."

She turned and looked in the direction Zahir was focused on. The sleek black car was identical to the other one, part of the royal fleet, she imagined. "You didn't drive, did you? Because you shouldn't drive."

He shot her a hard look. "I do not drive anymore. I should think the reason for that is quite obvious."

He jerked the back door open and she slid inside. He rounded the other side and sat next to her, his posture stiff. The driver pulled onto the road and turned back in the direction of the palace.

Katharine's heart was hammering hard, her hands shaking. Her entire body shaking, from the inside out. From the surge of adrenaline brought on by the whole situation, and from Zahir's nearness.

Silence filled the space between them. She waited as long as she could before all of the questions swirling in her mind had to escape her mouth.

"How often does it happen?" she asked.

He turned his head to look at her. "Much less frequently than it used to."

"It happened in your office last week."

He pushed his hand through his hair, a slight tremble visible to her, making her feel like she should look away. To let him regain his pride. To let him have back what he'd lost in that true, unguarded moment. But she couldn't.

"A short one." He didn't want to talk about it, she could see that. It was written in every tense line of muscle in his body. And yet she had to ask. She had to know.

"Are they...flashbacks?"

"It's the crowd," he said, his voice tight. "I saw...I thought you were in danger." He flexed his fingers before curling them back into a fist. "I'm not insane," he ground out.

"I know. I never thought you were." She played the moment over again, his eyes, his face, the true, deep fear in them. It had been real to him, what he had felt and seen. It hadn't been an overreaction or overprotection. It had been bone deep for him. "I... Is it posttraumatic stress? I've volunteered at a lot of hospitals in Austrich. Seen people who have been in accidents. It's common when someone has gone through something like you did."

He turned, angled away from her, his eyes on the passing scenery. "It probably is."

"Haven't you seen anyone?"

"They gave me medication to help me sleep. That's all."

She swallowed. "You don't take it, do you?"

He let out a short laugh. "Already you know me better than my doctors. No, I don't take it."

"Do you sleep?"

The corner of his lip curved up. "No."

"Maybe you should take..."

"No. Drugs to suppress it. To make me tired. What does that fix? Nothing. It just masks it. Another thing to control me when I…I should…I don't want this. I don't want to be affected by it," he said, his voice harsh.

She wanted to offer comfort, to touch him, and yet, she knew he would reject it. Reject her. "But you are."

"It's gotten better."

"That was not better."

He snorted. "Sure it was. You should have seen me at first. Ask Amarah how it was."

Her chest felt tight and she almost didn't want to ask the question. But she had to. "Who's Amarah?"

"She was my fiancée. She was there when I woke up, by my bedside. For all of five minutes before she turned and ran from the room. She came back, of course. She tried, for two days she tried, to deal with me, to help the doctors. But I would…I would black out. Or have a flashback and I was… unpredictable."

Katharine put her hand to her stomach, trying to calm the wave of nausea that washed through her. "Did you hurt her?"

He shook his head. "Never. I was trying to protect her but…how safe did you feel just now?" He laughed, a dark, humorless sound.

Katharine could see how Zahir might be frightening in that circumstance, but she had only been scared for him, not of him. She'd known, from the moment he'd pressed her up against the wall, that he was putting himself between her and whatever danger he thought was there.

That he'd been putting himself in harm's way. For her.

"Yes." It was honest, absolutely. "I felt safe with you."

He swallowed, his Adam's apple moving up and down. "Well, she didn't. And can you blame her? I didn't hurt her any of the times it happened. But if I lost too much of myself? If she were there during a night terror? When I imagined there were enemies all around? What would I have done to her then? Amarah was smart to leave."

Katharine didn't want to ask her next question either. "Do you miss her?"

He turned away from her. "I don't feel anything for her. About her." He looked back at her, his expression stoic, and she could see, from the flat look in his dark eyes, that it was true. He'd said he didn't feel love anymore. He didn't seem to regret the loss of it, either.

"Don't leave again," he said. "Not without telling me."

"I'll try to keep you in the loop, Zahir, but I couldn't find you. And I'm not a prisoner. Anyway, Kahlah knew and I had security with me. I know that doesn't keep you safe, not completely, but it's the best I can do. And I'm used to moving around freely."

"And now the entire country will know."

"That you were concerned for my safety," she said. "Nothing more. The truth of the matter is between us. Although, I think if people knew...I think they would understand."

"Some would," he said. "But here...there is a mix of old and new thought. Those out in the tribes, the bedouin... There are already rumors amongst the more traditional people that it was not Zahir who rose from the attacks, but the devil who now possesses him. I'm sure some of the people in the market believe it now. Or at least believe their Sheikh is insane, that my position as leader reflects a certain...weakness."

"Then we will show them otherwise."

"Katharine..."

"Why not, Zahir? Why not? You're going to have to handle the wedding."

"I *will* handle it," he said, his voice hard. "I am not a child."

"I know you aren't. I don't doubt your strength, not for one moment, and that's why I believe that you can take this and defeat it."

"As if I haven't tried?"

"You stay alone. Your solution has been ignoring it, and we found out today that doesn't work."

"It has. It did before you."

"But I'm here now." And part of her was sorry she was. Sorry she had burst into the order that Zahir had created for himself. Sorry for what she had done to his pride. He was strength, he embodied it, exuded it. Even in the moment when he'd been in the flashback, he had been bravery and honor, working to protect her above himself.

And she had exposed him to ridicule and shame.

"Yes, you are."

"What happened that day, Zahir?"

He tightened his jaw, then relaxed it, tendons in his neck shifting with the motion. "Read the articles about it."

"I have read the articles about it. I went to the funeral for your family, but I want you to tell me."

He shook his head. "I don't remember all of it and I can't… I can't remember it without seeing it. Like that. Like it was out there. I can't just remember it. I have to live it. Again and again."

The thought of that, of reliving that hell, made her feel cold all over. "All right. You don't have to tell me. But we can work on you going out."

"I've been out. I go to functions when my duty dictates I must."

Zahir fought against the rising rage that was filling him, threatening to drown him. To be seen in such a way…it was weakness beyond what was acceptable. He despised it. Despised that it lived in him. That it could overtake him.

That she had seen him that way. At his most vulnerable. That there was vulnerability in him… He had let his guard down. When he'd discovered her gone, when he'd found out where she went… Adrenaline had taken over, and from there it had broken down. The thin veil between the present and past rent, allowing the past to flood in.

Terror, pure and real, had filled him, and Katharine had been all he could see. *Save her. Save her.* It had pounded through him like a drumbeat, a constant directive, drowning out the terror, any concern for himself. It had been about her.

And then he'd seen her face, heard her voice, and the flood had receded.

"But the wedding will be more than that and...we need to go to Austrich. To be officially blessed in the Orthodox church. If not then we will not be legally married in the eyes of the people. Custom dictates it and my father has reminded me that it was a part of the original agreement."

The demand that it be altered was on the tip of his tongue and yet he could not bring himself to issue it. To do so would be to admit defeat. No one had asked him to do more than what he had been doing for the past five years. Everyone had been content to leave the Beast of Hajar in his cave, to wallow in his misery.

So long as the economy kept moving, nobody cared. And they didn't have to face the shame of a damaged ruler. Half of the people imagined him blessed by God. The others imagined him to be a demon. Most days he imagined the latter half was closer to the truth.

No one had challenged him...except for Katharine. She'd walked in challenging him and hadn't stopped since. His pride wouldn't allow him to turn her down. His pride also wouldn't allow him to go before a crowd of people and...lose himself like that.

The flashbacks were like waking nightmares. His subconscious taking control and forcing him to watch what he'd already experienced. He was still there, but the pictures in his mind...the memories...they made him feel what he'd felt that day. The acrid taste of panic on his tongue, the knowledge that he was powerless. The horrible, debilitating helplessness.

It took him right back to the worst moments of his life and forced him to not simply remember them, but to relive them.

The simplest thing had been to avoid anything and everything that might trigger the flashbacks. They had been hard to predict at first. A noise that was too loud, the scent of sulfur from a lit match, could all send him back down into hell. So it had been better if he simply stayed in the palace.

Even now that they had grown so few and far between, they weren't triggered by the obvious.

"It's the crowd," he said. He hated talking about it, liked explaining it even less, but it was preferable to her thinking he was crazy. "It's the last thing I truly remember of that day. We were driving through the city. It was a parade, a national celebration. So many people were there.

"And I noticed there was a crowd around the car…I thought they were just citizens but…there's always a barricade. By the time I realized it…"

He had to stop there. Had to. Because if he went too far into what had happened next, if he forced himself to remember, he would have to relive it. It was the way it worked.

"You couldn't have done anything different."

Such a tired refrain. One he had heard from every doctor, every visitor. He believed it no more from her than from any of them. "I could have died instead. Malik could have lived. It would have been better."

# CHAPTER SIX

KATHARINE let Zahir retreat to his quarters. Not that anyone really *let* Zahir do anything. He did what he pleased and he didn't seem to care what anyone thought. Least of all her.

Except for when it came to the flashbacks.

Her heart squeezed when she remembered that moment when he'd looked so frightened, so lost. How he had protected her, his instinct to save her, even through that fear. He had placed himself between her and the world, and it had been instinct.

*I could have died instead.*

He hadn't spoken those words like a man looking for sympathy, or one out to shock. It had been steady, matter-of-fact. And that's what had made it truly frightening. Because it was obvious he had thought them before. Obvious that he believed them.

Things had moved on in her life. Austrich had changed, she had taken on new projects, found different ways she could serve. But in Hajar, time seemed to have stood still.

And Zahir with it.

No, maybe that wasn't true. He had changed. He had grown so dark, so bitter. Lost in his own personal hell, and no one had come to retrieve him from it.

A sharp twinge of anger stabbed her in the chest. She couldn't fathom how his fiancée could leave him like she had.

She would have stayed with Malik, and she hadn't even loved him. Because she'd made a promise. And promises mattered, commitment and honor mattered. At least to her they did.

What would have happened if Amarah had stayed? Well, Zahir might not have Amarah, but he had her. And she had given her word to him now that she would be his wife. And even if she was a temporary wife, she would do whatever it took to be there for him. To build a strong union. They needed it for their countries.

Katharine made her way toward Zahir's quarters, her footsteps too loud in the empty corridor. It was late, and the staff was gone, which added to the cavernous feeling the palace possessed. It didn't escape her that she was always the one looking for him. That he had only come to her room once, and that was to tell her to leave.

But the distance between them didn't seem right. Not when they were supposed to be working together. It especially didn't seem right after today.

She pushed open the door and found the gym area vacant, which she'd expected. She walked through, brushing her fingers along one of the exercise machines as she did. His body was strong, he worked at it, intensely. To show no weakness.

She'd forced him to show weakness twice in the same week.

The thought made her feel sick.

There was a short corridor in between the gym and Zahir's room. His room was empty too, not just of him, but of almost anything. There was a bed in the corner, a large armoire and very little else.

There was a chin-up bar in the doorway that led outside into the courtyard. Something else physical for him to do. He seemed to need the outlet.

She looked at the bed, pillows pushed to the side, the bedspread and sheets tangled. He had been here. And he hadn't been able to sleep. He'd said he couldn't sleep. She felt the twinge in her chest again.

She walked across the room and bent over the bed, tugging the bedding into place and arranging the pillows again. It was an idle thing to do, something to keep her hands busy while she decided what to do next. But it was her way of trying to put something in his life back together. Since she'd come in guns blazing and torn it apart.

*It was torn apart already. You did what you had to do. And anyway, it isn't as though you forced him.*

No. He'd agreed. Because it was the right thing to do. Because duty was important, honor. It mattered. It had to, otherwise her whole life had been geared toward…nothing. It was the only thing she knew how to do. The only thing that gave her purpose.

"What are you doing?"

Katharine turned sharply and saw Zahir standing in the doorway that led outside, his chest bare and glistening with a light sheen of sweat in the pale moonlight.

"I just came to…"

"You cannot leave me alone, can you, Katharine?" The words were torn from him, a desperation laced through them that shocked and frightened her.

"How can I? After what you said?" she asked, her pulse pounding in her temples, making her feel dizzy.

"Easily. Leave me be as everyone else has done for the past five years. I agreed to a marriage on paper only because I wanted to ignore you as much as humanly possible." He growled the words, rough sounding and feral, the rage behind them barely leashed.

"Why did you agree to it at all?"

"Because it is best for my people. I may not be able to go out in a crowd of them, but that doesn't lessen my responsibility here."

"I…I'm sorry about today."

He moved into the room, his body taking up an amazing amount of space in the cavernous surroundings. "You're sorry about today, sorry about the table. Is that what you're here for? To show me just how sorry you are?"

He wrapped an arm around her waist and pulled her to him. He leaned in, his lips skimming the curve of her neck. Katharine felt her legs start to shake, not from fear, from something else. From the attraction that had assaulted her off and on from the moment she'd seen him in his office.

Even now. With all of his rage directed at her, she felt something else vibrating between them. Something even more powerful.

"Have you come to show me how sorry you are with that beautiful body of yours?" he whispered the words, his lips touching her earlobe lightly, a slight tremor in his fingers. "How appropriate. A virgin sacrifice to appease the Beast." He flexed his hand, fingers spreading wide on her waist, his thumb brushing the underside of her breast. Her breath caught in her throat. She wanted him to let her go. And she wanted him to pull her tightly into his body.

He stayed like that, his face so close to hers, his breath feathering against her cheek, hot and intimate. He slid his finger over the line of her jaw, the gesture so gentle and subtle, at odds with the rage vibrating from him. Rage was the surface emotion, but when she looked in his eyes, she saw something else. Need. So raw and real it was a palpable force.

He dropped his arm from her waist, pulling back sharply, the sudden shock of cold as the distance widened between them making goose bumps break out on her arms.

"I don't need your pity," he spat, taking another step back.

Anger boiled in Katharine's stomach, anger and unsatisfied desire, and she had no idea what business either of them had existing beside the other. Although, it seemed it was the same for Zahir. That, at least, provided its own satisfaction.

Zahir's eyes were cold on her, glittering in the dim room.

"You don't have my pity," she said tightly. "I'm sorry for what happened to your family, I'm sorry that you had to go through it. No man, no woman, no one, should ever have to see the things you've seen. But right now, you're just a jackass. And I don't pity a man who acts like a jackass just because he thinks he can get away with it. We're getting married in eight weeks. I'm willing to help you. But no matter what you choose, you need to think of a way to civilize yourself. And the flashbacks have nothing to do with that."

Zahir watched Katharine turn on her heel and stride from the room, her posture stiff, her footsteps hard and loud on the marble floor.

A flood of regret, so real and unfiltered it shocked him, filled him. He gritted his teeth against anger, and the painful arousal that was still making its presence felt.

Five years and he hadn't felt the slightest twinge of sexual desire. Nothing. But Katharine had brought it roaring to life the first time she'd come into his office. And when he'd come in from his ride in the desert he'd seen her, bending over his bed, her tight butt on display for him, looking like every man's perfect fantasy…it had been too much.

The need to take her, to push her onto the bed and shove that little dress up around her hips…it had been so strong he'd honestly wondered if he stood a chance of resisting. It had tugged at his control, tearing the threads of it, leaving a mangled mass of desire and lust.

Before, he would have showed his interest. He would have seduced her, and he would have been confident in her desire for him. He'd been a playboy, at least until he'd met Amarah. And women had been easy to come by. Willing and fun, giving of their bodies and pleasure, as he gave of his.

But the man he was now... If there was even a woman willing to bed the Beast, a woman who roused his desire, he would deny it. Because as important as sex and release had been then, control was needed now.

And Katharine had shaken it. If he gave in to the lust, threw off the shackles he had willingly locked onto himself, he didn't know what might happen.

If she wanted to heal him, she was welcome to it. The truth was, he did have to stand up at their wedding without being assaulted by flashbacks. And he would do it. He wasn't foolish enough to think it was a simple matter of being strong enough, though he wished it were. It went beyond that. But he would do what he had to.

He would master it. And he would master his feelings for her.

There was no other option.

"What is it you propose we do?" he asked, walking into the courtyard the next morning.

Katharine was already there, her hair pulled up into a neat bun, a cup of coffee frozen midway between the table and her mouth as she looked up at him, green eyes owlishly wide. She set the mug down. "Excuse me?"

"What is it you propose we do to stop the flashbacks. You seemed to have an idea yesterday?"

"And you seemed to be on the verge of throwing me out of the palace last night."

"That was last night."

"And so it doesn't matter?"

He waved a hand in dismissal of her words. "Not anymore." He was moving past it. Past that strong wave of lust and the anger that had been tangled up in it. He was ready to fight now, like the warrior he was. The warrior that had been lost in the guise of a king for the past five years. Control wasn't enough. He had to strike out, take the things holding him back by the throat and crush them.

"It does matter. Because it matters to me. I'm not your enemy, Zahir. Your enemies have been dealt with, haven't they?"

He nodded curtly. Those memories were clear. The men who had thrown grenades beneath his family's motorcade had been dealt with in the harshest terms the laws allowed.

"I am not one of them. I'm not fighting against you. I'm fighting for my country, for yours. For my brother. And I need a man who is capable of being a strong Regent for Austrich."

"I am capable. More than. Have you taken a look at the progress that has been made in Hajar since I was appointed?"

"Of course I have. I've known…" She averted her eyes. "I've known for a while now that there was a possibility I might have to marry you. I've been paying attention to what you were doing."

"While avoiding ever seeing me."

"It's not like you're renowned for your lavish and lively parties."

"Point taken."

"And I was ignoring this part of my job," she said.

"Job?"

"Don't you consider being Sheikh a job?"

"Of the most demanding variety. Paperwork that never seems to end, and constant…trivial-seeming things that take every last moment of time," he said.

"And it's the same for me, even if my responsibilities are different. Marriage was always in the job description. Marriage to forge alliances, at the very least, at most for the reason we're marrying."

"But you were ignoring it?"

"Yes. When it was delayed I…took the delay. For as long

as I could. In truth, I left it too long because I waited until we were at a crisis point. It was wrong of me."

"It was better that you did. Wait, that is, because it was your crisis that decided for me."

"It was?"

"Trade is one thing. It's advantageous, of course, and it's important. But I could not condemn your country to civil war. To more spilled blood. I could not face having more on my hands." He flexed his hands into fists as he said it. He felt the stains there. He should have been able to stop it. At the very least, he should have shielded his brother.

"There isn't any blood on your hands, Zahir. I'm not your enemy, and you're not the enemy, either."

"Enough," he said, shutting the door on the discussion. On the memories. He couldn't afford to think about it now, to lose focus. "Back to the original reason I'm here. How do you plan on preparing me for the wedding?"

"I have a few ideas."

She met his eyes; they were so deep, so lovely and green. Still so filled with emotion and possibility.

"We'll beat this. We're going to keep fighting."


"Ready?" Katharine looked at Zahir's strong profile and she knew that there was no way he would ever claim to not be ready. His pride wouldn't permit it.

"Yes."

Which told her nothing because she'd already known what his answer would be. "Good."

The driver pulled the car forward and out of the palace, heading toward the city center. "It isn't as though I don't travel," he said.

"I know you do. A little bit. And I also know you avoid driving near places like the market, where people might crowd the car."

"I'm not afraid," he said, his words short. Clipped.

"I never said you were."

"You think it. There is nothing for me to be afraid of. I have faced death and if it came again, I would fight it, and if I couldn't fight it, I would embrace it. What I don't like is having my mind taken over. Having no control over what I see. Over what I do. I would much more happily face death." His entire body was tense, each muscle tightened. "Do you know what it's like…to have to spend so much energy keeping the demons at bay? To never have one moment of peace? I relive it. Daily. Not to the degree you witnessed in the market, but it is never truly gone."

She swallowed, her throat tight. "Why?"

"I…I have to remember it," he said, his voice rough.

"No, Zahir, you don't."

"Everyone is dead, Katharine. Malik, my mother, my father, the guards in the motorcade who were there to protect us. How can I let it go? Should I get over it? They never will. They're gone."

The pain in his words burned into her, marking her. In that moment, she understood. He carried the memory of his family's last moments because he felt that not doing so would diminish the tragedy. She understood, because she felt like she had to shoulder some of his pain. That she had to share. So he wouldn't be alone.

"They are gone," she said softly. "But you're here. And I need you. Your people need you. And that's why you'll beat it."

He focused on his palms. "I thought I had." He looked away. "No, I knew I had not. But I thought I had them managed. The two I've had since you've arrived were the first true flashbacks I've had in over a year."

She tried to force a laugh. "So…it's me then."

Dark eyes locked with hers. "You make it hard to concentrate, that much is true. And yet somehow—" he looked away again "—your voice…your face…brought me back."

Emotion rose in her fast and fierce like a tide. "Good. We'll go with that." She rested her hand on the seat between them. "Hold on to me if you feel it coming."

He looked down at her hand, a dark eyebrow arched, his expression filled with pure, masculine stubbornness. It was welcome compared to the bleak, grief-stricken look that had come over him when he'd spoken of his family. "I will block it out."

"If it were that simple that's what you would always do."

His expression was fierce. "It should be that simple. I should be stronger."

"You should be stronger? You should bear all this weight and somehow heal at the same time? How should you be stronger, Zahir? You survived. Not only that, you're ruling your country in a way that would make your father and Malik so proud."

"They were made for this life. They were born to it. Men of diplomacy, men of the people." He laughed, a sound that was cold and humorless. Laced with a kind of bitter pain that was so real and unvarnished it hurt to hear it. "We both know I am not a diplomat, to say the least."

"You care for your people. Just because you don't spend your life in the public eye doesn't mean you don't. Just because it isn't as easy for you doesn't mean you don't do just as well as Malik would have."

"Why exactly do you want to fix me, *latifa*?" he asked, ignoring her earlier words.

There it was again. Beauty. The entire sentence was dripping with insincerity, and yet she found herself clinging to that one word, turning it over. She'd been called beautiful so many times, mostly by the press. The same press that might turn around and call her ugly the next day if she wore a shade of yellow that didn't flatter her skin tone. It had never mattered. If the insult could be a lie, so could the compliment.

Her father used it, too. Sincerely, and yet it always seemed to undermine any value she had as a person. It had become an annoyance. A near insult in its own right.

But for some reason, hearing it from Zahir's lips made something happen inside of her. A warm kind of tingling that spread through her body, pooling low in her stomach.

She blinked and looked up at him, into his flat, black eyes. "I…because I have to. The wedding. We have to show strength."

Her words were clumsy. And they were wrong. There was so much more to this now, to what she was feeling. But she didn't know what else to say. Always, she had worked for her country's betterment. Even her time in the hospitals had been in service of their military men. She didn't really know how to separate what she wanted from what she was supposed to do.

Except for those light-at-the-end-of-the-tunnel moments where she had some vague, exhilarating sense of freedom. Whatever that meant.

Although now, sitting with Zahir, even with the tension and sadness, she felt peace. A kind of peace she never felt.

The car turned, taking the more densely populated route that would lead them into the heart of the city. She sensed Zahir tensing next to her and stretched her hand out so that her fingertips rested against his. She'd said the wrong thing, but the physical touch seemed like the right thing.

And he accepted it.

The road narrowed and became more crowded with vehicle and foot traffic as they neared the market, and everything slowed to a crawl. She could sense Zahir's anxiety as the people closed in on the car, weaving around them so they could cross the street.

"Look at me," she said.

He turned his head, his forehead glossed with sweat, his jaw set tight.

"Look at me," she said again. "I'm here. So are you."

His hand drifted closer to hers until it engulfed it, his thumb lightly moving over her knuckles. He tightened his hold on her for a moment, then released, then squeezed again. Her chest felt tight, too tight. Watching him fight like he was, she felt like she was seeing strength beyond anything she'd ever witnessed. Because he was battling inner demons that went well beyond what most men would be asked to face. Beyond what anyone should ever be asked to endure.

"I don't really know what I'm doing," she said softly.

"Just keep doing it," he said, his teeth gritted. "Because it seems to be working."

Her throat tightened. She was angry. So angry that he was dealing with this. That someone had done this to him. And she didn't know what sort of help or hope she could offer.

"What did you do last night?" she asked.

He blew out a breath, his jaw loosening slightly. "Caught an intruder in my bedroom."

She felt the corners of her mouth tug up into a smile. "Before that."

"I was riding. My horse. She makes up for what I can't see. And while there are cars with the technology to help with that…it isn't the same."

"No, it couldn't be. Animals have an intuition that technology can't possess. I like to ride, too." She took a breath. Took a chance. "I'd like to go out with you. Riding, I mean."

He nodded slowly. "In the evening sometime," he said. "When it isn't too hot."

"I'd like that."

They were through the center of town, through the crowd of people. He relaxed, pulling his hand away and placing it in his lap.

"Are you ready to go back?" she asked, wondering if they'd pushed hard enough for the day.

"I'm fine," he said.

And she knew that he meant it.

# CHAPTER SEVEN

ZAHIR stopped in the doorway of the library. Katharine was there, sitting by the fireplace, an orange glow bathing the pages of her book, and her pale skin. The fire wasn't really necessary, even though the desert did get cooler at night. But he had a feeling Katharine had lit it for ambiance, comfort. She was that kind of person. The kind who enjoyed moments, small, simple things. Like flowers in vases.

When it didn't irritate him, it amazed him. Made him ache for something he didn't truly believe he could ever find for himself.

It made him feel like he should turn away from her. To go back to where things were numb.

But he didn't want to. For the moment, he would take the ache with the pleasure of seeing her. "Come riding with me."

She looked up at him, a smile spreading over her face. "I'd love to." She stood from the chair she'd been sitting in and set her book on the side table.

It did strange things to his stomach, to have her say she wanted to do something with him. And she smiled at him. Very few people smiled at him.

But then, Katharine was like very few people.

"Not in that," he said, looking at the brief sundress she was wearing. It was her standard uniform, and one he wouldn't complain about, because he could look at her legs all day, but it wasn't workable riding gear. Even if the thought did make his blood pump faster, hotter than it had in years.

"I'll change."

She walked past him and his eyes were drawn down to the shapely curve of her hips as they swayed with each step. Fierce hunger gripped him, lust tightening into his stomach like metal hooks, digging deep, painfully so.

He wanted her with a need that defied logic. A need that defied reality. Katharine had an untouchable beauty, ethereal and earthy at the same time. The kind a man could only dream of tasting once in his life.

The kind he could never touch.

And she was to be his wife. But not his wife in any true sense of the word. A woman still so far out of his reach, she might as well be back in her own country. A woman he had no right to touch.

He'd been crazy to force her to stay in Austrich as part of the arrangement. At the time, he'd been trying to punish her. Now he could see it was only punishing him.

She had offered herself to him once, offered to have a marriage with him on whatever terms he desired. Right now, he desired whatever terms would make stripping her of that little dress and losing himself in her body acceptable.

"Just a second," she said, slipping into her room and closing the door behind her.

He rested his palm, still raw from the day he'd fallen into the broken vase shards, on the cold, painted wood of the door. It was a poor substitute for the warm, soft flesh of a woman. But it would have to do.

It had been so long since he'd touched a woman's skin. But he would rather live as a monk for the rest of his life than force a woman into his bed. Not physically, and not through manipulation. He would have a partner who desired him. An impossible desire, perhaps. Pride still lived in him, as much as his injuries would allow. That, and humanity. He would never sink to such a base level. He might be known as a Beast, but he was still a man. No amount of sexual frustration would strip him of that.

He curled his fingers in, making a fist that still rested against the cool surface of the door. He was a man. He would not use her need for marriage, her altruistic intentions to save her country, to get her into bed.

But he was tempted. So much he shook with it. Tempted to disregard what she might want, how she might feel about him, what letting his guard down to that degree might do to both of them, and think of his desire alone.

"Ready." She opened the door and stepped out in a pair of figure-hugging sand-colored leggings and a structured olive-green jacket. It was like the runway version of a riding outfit. Fitted, sleek and eye-catching.

It was also the antithesis of a solution as far as getting his libido reined in was concerned.

"Come out this way." He started to head out toward the back of the palace, the exit that was nearest the stables, where the horses were waiting, already tacked up.

He looked down at her hand and was tempted to take it in his. As he had done yesterday. She had been his anchor then. Had kept him from slipping over into that abyss that always came just before his mind was assaulted by violent flashbacks.

He tightened his hand into a fist and denied the impulse, letting her simply follow him.

"I haven't been out to the stables yet. I didn't…I wasn't really sure if it might be off-limits to me."

"And yet you find my bedroom a nice place to pass time in the evening."

"Well, I was looking for you. And I…I know I've made a mess of some things here, Zahir."

"The mess was already made, Katharine," he said, having to force his words through his tightened throat. "Why do you do that?"

"Why do I do what?"

"For a woman with such confidence, you seem to take on more than your share of fault."

"I just…I want to be useful."

"Is that all?"

She was silent then, no witty comeback to that response. For the first time, he felt sorry for her. She was doing what she felt was right, what she felt she had to do, and yet, by her own admission, this experience was comparable to being in a darkened tunnel. And she was waiting for the light. That moment when she could be free. Of all this. Of him. Of the disaster that he was.

"Perhaps," she said, finding her witty comeback, he assumed, "you see it in me because the same tendency lives in you."

"I have earned every ounce of my guilt."

"No," she said, "you haven't. The guilt belongs to other men, Zahir. The men who attacked your family. All for what?"

"Money," he said. "Power."

"All things you don't seem to care about. Or even want. I don't see how you think you have a stake in this."

"Because I am left. I had to have committed a sin to manage that," he said.

"Or maybe you were blessed."

"That's the last thing I feel, *latifa*."

He opened the door to the outside and relished the feel of the cool evening wind on his face. This was when he felt normal. Alive. Otherwise he just felt…nothing, either that or a crippling guilt. Well, he could add lust to the list now. Nothing, guilt and lust. It was a small step, but it was a step.

The horses, one bay and one black, were waiting just outside the barn, tethered to the fence. He walked over to the larger, black mare and stroked her nose. The horses didn't fear him. "This is Lilah. You can ride her. She's very gentle."

"The sentiment is appreciated, but I don't need gentle."

That statement made a dark cascade of erotic thoughts spin through his mind, made him pause for a moment as he thought of all the hidden meanings her statement could possess.

"Noted," he said, jaw clenched tight.

"And who's your handsome gentleman there?" she asked.

He put his foot in the stirrup and swung his leg over his mount. "Nalah doesn't appreciate being called a he."

"Sorry. I assumed—" she pulled herself up onto Lilah "—that a big strong man like you would ride a stallion."

"Oh, no, definitely not. Not a good idea to have two stallions together, you know?"

She laughed, a shocked burst of sound that echoed through the paddock. "Did you just call yourself a stallion?"

He felt a smile teasing the edges of his lips, such a foreign feeling, even more so the small bit of contentment that accompanied it. Such a strange thing to talk to another person like this. To find that barrier of fear and uncertainty absent. Pride grew in him, mingling with the surge of warmth that was trickling through his veins. He had made her smile, after she had looked so sad.

"I did," he said.

"Mmm…quite the ego."

"If you can beat me to that last fence post over there, the one just in front of the large rock formation, you might just put a dent in it."

She grinned at him and urged Lilah on with her feet, not waiting for further word from him. Fine as far as he was concerned. He could watch her shapely backside rise and fall with the motion of the horse, and then pass her at the end, of that he had no doubt. He couldn't drive safely, couldn't walk without a limp, but on the back of a horse, things were seamless. Easy.

The sand pounded beneath Nalah's hooves, a beat that resounded in his body, in his soul. It made him feel complete. Healed in some ways. The sun dipped completely behind one of the few flat mountains that dotted the Hajari skyline and bathed everything in a purple glow.

He could still see Katharine clearly, pale ankles and face visible in the dim lighting. She had such a delicate look to her, and yet nothing could be further from the truth. Delicate, she was not. She was strength personified.

But she wasn't going to win the race.

He overtook her at the last moment with ease and she let out a short, sharp curse word when she came to a stop just behind him, her hair wild around her face, her breathing labored, cheeks flushed pink.

"Oh, you knew you were going to do that, didn't you?" she said, gasping and laughing at the same time.

"Of course I did." He slid off of Nalah, grimacing as pain shot through his thigh when his feet made contact with the hard ground. The sand was thinner here, the terrain a bit rockier, and his muscle noticed the lack of extra cushion.

Katharine dismounted, too, and shook her main of coppery hair out, sending the faint scent of vanilla into the air, into him. It was like a sucker punch straight to his gut.

"Fair enough. If we'd been on my home turf, I would have done the same to you."

"Speaking of home turf," he said, ignoring the tightness of desire that was making itself felt at the apex of his thighs, drowning out any muscle pain he'd been experiencing. "I want to show you something."

This hadn't been part of the plan, but now that they were here it seemed logical somehow. She would want to see this.

She'd been connected to Malik, too. There were so few people in his life that were.

There were so few people in his life, full stop. But it suddenly made sharing this seem vital. If someone else knew, then the memory would have a better chance at living. And maybe it wouldn't feel quite so heavy on him.

He led Nalah to the post and tethered her to it, more of a precaution than he probably needed to take, but he didn't chance things with his horses. Katharine followed his lead.

"All right, lead the way."

"This way."

Katharine followed Zahir, her heart still pounding, from the exhilaration of the ride, and from the intense adrenaline high that came just from being with him. Zahir was an experience all on his own. Infuriating, fascinating, arousing. She'd never known anyone like him.

Certainly Malik hadn't been like this. He'd been fun. Easygoing. Truthfully, five years ago Zahir hadn't even been like that. He'd been more of an enigma, always a bit more serious than his brother, but nothing like the man she'd got to know over the past week.

She followed him to the outcropping of rocks that seemed to have been placed there, everything around it flat and desolate for miles.

There was a small space between the rocks, just big enough for them to pass through.

"What is this?" she asked, looking at the green surroundings. The rocks curved inward and offered partial shade, and water trickled down the side of the natural walls.

"*Amal*, the Oasis of Hope. This was what drew the first band of my people here to Kadim. Hajar is mostly flat and shelter from the elements is hard to find. They had been walking through the desert for weeks with no reprieve, and they found this outcropping. There was water, shelter."

"And eventually a palace nearby. And a city," she finished.

"The city came first. But this has always been a special place to my family. Malik and I used to come here as boys. A place we could play, escape the heat and the indoors."

She could picture them as they'd been. Boys with no cares. "Things must have seemed simpler then."

He shrugged. "Yes and no. I always knew. Always knew that Malik had a heavy burden to carry. I was always grateful that it wasn't me." He laughed, the sound cold and flat in the enclosed space. "I have wondered…" He looked down, then back at her. "I have wondered if that's why I'm left. A trick of fate. I was always much more content with my lot. So happy that it was my brother who bore the responsibility of leadership." He cleared his throat. "I was a military officer. I should have seen the signs. I should have known."

She touched his forearm. "You should have known what?"

"I should have known what was coming. I've seen war. Usually, I…feel things in my gut. That day, there was nothing. I was blindsided. We all were. And I was the only one who had no excuse. It never should have got past me."

"You couldn't have known, Zahir."

"I know," he said harshly. "I know." He softened his tone. "But sometimes I still think I should have been able to stop it."

"No. The only people who could have stopped it are the ones who did it. They could have turned back that day. They didn't."

"All for power. Fools. Power is an empty thing."

"Not if you use it right."

"And spare few do. Power, the lust of it, is why you're here and not at home. Why you have to guard Alexander. Because of people who will do anything to get it."

"So it's the ones who don't want it who do best with it. That's why you're such a good leader, Zahir."

"And what about you, Katharine the Great?" She arched

her brow at the nickname and he pressed on. "What about you and all the responsibility you take on? Is it your job to fix everyone?"

"Yes. Maybe. I don't know what else to do. Unlike you, I do feel called to rule. And yet I can't. I never will. I have to... do something. Find a way to...matter. And if I fix things to accomplish it, then okay. I'll be the one to fix things."

He looked at her for a long time, his dark eyes assessing her, causing prickles of heat to fire beneath her skin, making her want to close the gap between them, then share her warmth. Because he looked cold, and she wanted so badly to make the cold go away for him.

"You do not need to fix me," he said, his voice flat.

Suddenly she realized she didn't know how. She offered him platitudes. They were even true, but they weren't... enough. She'd been taught to lead with her head, and it wasn't enough with Zahir. She wanted to put a bandage on it and call it better, when she doubted if that were even possible.

She looked at him standing there, a warrior, even if he was a warrior scarred by battle. The scars inside were so much worse than the ones that covered his skin. And she had the swirling, helpless sensation of knowing she wouldn't be enough for him. That she would never be able to reach him.

"It was easier today," Zahir said, entering the library.

Katharine set her book aside and treated him to one of her easy smiles, a sight he'd become more accustomed to than he should have. More than he'd like to admit.

"I'm glad."

The drive into town today had been easier. They had been getting progressively so. The touch of Katharine's hand, her face, they anchored him. Kept him in the present. Ironic since he had attributed the flashbacks to her, to his losing control.

The wedding was another matter. Hundreds of people

with their eyes trained on them, the chance for him to either emerge in triumph, or humiliate his people. His family name. It was hard to explain, even to himself, what he thought might happen in that situation. The possibility of lost time, a loss of control, with an audience, was more terrifying and more likely than the chance of another attack.

And that he had control over. At least he was finding he did. That there were touchstones he could reach out to. That Katharine's voice could keep the gates that held back the memories locked up tight. That there were things other than the exhausting, all-consuming use of his self-will to keep himself from experiencing them in crowded spaces.

"The wedding will be easy," he said.

"Easy?" She pushed up out of the chair and stood, arms folded. He allowed himself a tour of her curves, welcomed the tightening of lust in his gut. "Weddings are never easy, no matter what the circumstances."

"I thought you were trying to make me feel better about all this."

"I'm just trying to get us through," she said.

"A lofty goal."

"I think it's all any engaged couple can hope for."

"You may have a point there," he said. "Although my first engagement was brief."

"Oh…Amarah."

The venom in her tone amused him. "Amarah wasn't evil."

"I can't imagine her as anything else," she said. "She should have stayed with you."

"So you didn't end up having to deal with me?"

"No. Because she made a promise to you."

He gritted his teeth, hating to tell the story, yet feeling he had to. So she could understand. "You remember how I was the first time in the market." She nodded. "I was like that all the time after. Moments of lucidity followed by endless screaming, raging. I was in pain, and the medication I was given to manage either made me sleep or made reality become blurred. I was not the man she knew. I didn't even look like the man she knew. The skin on my face was so badly burned I wasn't recognizable. And for a while they thought my mind was gone, too. I thought it was. There was so much grief. So much pain everywhere, inside of me, my skin felt like it was still on fire. And when I started to shut it down, my memories, my emotions, then I could function. Then I could learn to walk, learn to deal with losing the vision in my eye. How could I have asked her to stay? How could I have asked her to live with the Beast?"

"You aren't…"

"I was. Then especially." He had never spoken these words to anyone. Never told the whole truth of it. But he wanted her to know.

Her green eyes were filled with pain. Not pity. Nothing so condescending. It was as though she felt what he'd felt. As though she shared in it. "How did you even go on, though? To lose your family…and then her?"

"I had Hajar. And I knew that I had to protect my people. That it was left to me. And as much as I am not a ruler…I had to do what I could. I started with homeland security, moved into hospitals for children who had been victims of attacks. We treat children from all over the world for free. Of course to support that I had to work on new ways of bringing revenue in. It's kept me going."

"How can you think you aren't meant to be a ruler, Zahir? Your people…"

"Are afraid of me."

"Maybe because you haven't shown them who you really are."

She said it with such earnest sweetness, as though she truly believed there was something in him worth valuing, even after his admission of how…dark and empty he was inside. Maybe she just didn't understand. He'd been told that could be part of the PTSD, too. The absence of emotion. But it didn't go away. Other things had gotten better, but the blank void inside him remained. And knowing that it might have a medical cause did nothing to make it less acute.

He looked at her, studied the way she looked at him. And he longed to change it. He turned away from her. "So I have been preparing to deal with the crowd. Is there anything else?"

"We…we'll have to dance. We don't have to dance, actually. If your leg…"

His stomach tightened. He'd been damned if he'd take the easy way, the handicap or whatever it was she was offering. "I thought we had to."

"Not if you…I don't want to…"

"You told me you're not fragile. Neither am I," he said. "I used to dance. I didn't take lessons or anything, but especially during my university years in Europe, I danced quite a bit." Not that he'd enjoyed it for its own sake. It had been more of a pickup technique. But it had worked.

"That surprises me."

"It shouldn't. Women like to dance and I always liked women."

"And they liked you."

"It seems another lifetime ago, but if I can ride a horse, I'm certain I can dance. Unless you don't want to dance with a man who might limp through the steps."

She frowned. "That's not it. I don't want to tax you, I…"

A shot of competitiveness sent a spark of adrenaline through him. "*Latifa*, you are welcome to try to tax me. I doubt you will be able to."

A stubborn spark lit her eye, an answer to his challenge. Good. He wanted her to challenge him. To see him as a man, and not her patient. "I'd like to see some of these dancing skills," she said.

"Not up to par with what you're used to, I'm certain. But I know I still can."

He held out his hand and she simply stared at it. "I'm not really used to anything. I haven't done a lot of dancing."

"That surprises me."

"Why?"

"You're a beautiful woman."

Katharine cleared her throat and looked away, the compliment making her feel self-conscious. "Well, I am a woman who was promised to a sheikh in marriage. And who anticipated being used for another political union so...I was never really encouraged to dance."

"And you need encouragement to do things? I thought you did as you pleased."

"I do what my father asks," she said quietly. "What makes him see some kind of value in me."

Zahir's eyebrows locked together, his expression fierce. He leaned in, cupping her chin and tilting her face up so that she had to look at him. "If he does not see the value in you, he is a blind fool. No, not even blind. I can't see out of one eye, and yet I see your value."

Katharine swallowed hard, her eyes riveted to his. "Do you?"

"You are the only person who has challenged me, on this side of the attack or the other. You have more tenacity than any man I have ever met."

"Same goes," she said, fighting to keep from crying, to keep from melting over the words he'd just spoken. They were balm on a wound she hadn't realized was so raw. "Now," she said, trying to change the topic before she dissolved, "dance with me."

Eyes trained on her, Zahir bent and picked up a flat remote from the side table, pointing it upward and hitting one of the buttons. Slow, sexy jazz guitar filled the air. Not what she expected against the Arabic backdrop, but maybe even more fitting because of that. Because none of this was what she expected.

Zahir advanced on her slowly, his black eyes on hers, his movements languid, despite the limp. He held out his hand and she took it, warmth flooding her when his fingers entwined with hers. He pulled her to him, her breasts meeting his chest, and he wound his other arm around her waist. For a moment she saw it, the playboy he'd been. The man who'd had women falling at his feet, into his bed.

It coupled with the other things she knew about him, the intensity of the trauma he'd undergone. How far he had come since. As sexy as he had been before the attacks, as attractive as he'd been when he'd been a playboy dancing his way through the clubs in Europe, she knew that Zahir couldn't touch the man he was now.

This Zahir possessed a fire. An intensity. He had clawed over every obstacle in his path. He had emerged with a strength and honor that made her feel so safe with him. That made her respect him in ways she'd never respected another human being.

And on top of all that, when he held her to the heat of his body, she felt a kind of desire she'd never even dreamed possible.

It made her shivery inside.

His movements weren't completely smooth, his limp impossible to disguise entirely. But he had rhythm, more naturally than she did. Then, as she'd told Zahir, she hadn't done a lot of dancing. This made her wish she had. Made her wish she'd pursued a little more than what duty asked of her.

This was a layer of life she'd never explored. She was starting to fear that there were many of them. Beneath that thin layer of what royal life offered her, there was so much more. A richness and depth she'd never yet reached.

She'd never been conscious of it before.

He moved his hand from her lower back, around to the curve of his hip, his fingers tightening there, gripping her. She looked up, met his dark gaze. She didn't want to turn away.

She tightened her arms around his neck, bringing herself in closer. Needing to be closer. Needing to simply be near him. Needing something even more than that, and not quite knowing how to get it.

This wasn't part of the plan. Any plan. Human touch, human warmth, was unfamiliar to her. And right now, Zahir was hot. And so very close.

She unclasped her hands and wove her fingers through his thick, black hair. A deep rumble echoed in his chest, his eyes hot on hers.

She slid her hand forward, up the side of his neck, cupping his cheek, his skin rough from stubble beneath her palm. She needed more. She needed closer. Needed to satisfy the empty well of longing that had opened up in her. A well she was afraid might be impossible to fill.

But she could try. She had to try.

She stretched up on her toes, pressing her lips lightly against his. It was like an electric shock, the current starting where their mouths met and skittering through her veins, sending a shot of adrenaline straight to her heart.

He was still beneath her lips, his fingers curling around the skirt of her dress, the material bunching in his fist. The rumble turned to a growl, low and feral. Sexy on a level she'd never imagined something like that could be.

Granted, her experience with men and kissing was limited. So limited it could almost be called nonexistent. Because she'd known that she would have to marry for her country. For many traditional leaders a virgin bride would be expected. It had been written into the contract hers and Malik's fathers had signed.

She wondered why she'd stood for that now. Why she'd calmly let them decree something like that. Something so personal and *hers*. Because it had seemed right then. Like she had to do the best thing for Austrich, and if that meant not ever having a real relationship of her choosing...

She had done that. Sacrificed ever pursuing a man she was interested in because of a marriage contract drawn up six years ago.

The realization was obvious, but stunning. The sudden understanding of what personal, private things in her life had been controlled by those she trusted.

No one was making her do this. She wanted this.

She deepened the kiss, parting her lips and sliding her tongue over the outline of his top lip, over the slashing scar that ran through it. He shuddered beneath the touch, every muscle in his back shivering beneath her fingertips.

He tightened his hold on her, brought her tight against his body. She could feel his erection pressing firmly against her stomach. She broke the kiss to suck in a sharp breath and he took advantage, pressing a kiss to the hollow of her throat, the curve of her neck. Teeth nipping, his tongue soothing.

He moved his hands from her hips to her waist, his hold tight, but good. She loved the intensity of it, him clinging to her as though she was bringing him life, as though she were water in the desert.

He was to her. His touch, his mouth. It was heady, intoxicating, far beyond anything she'd ever imagined possible. It was like having a veil torn from her eyes, seeing everything clearly for the first time.

Seeing how little she'd truly felt in her life.

She turned her head and captured his mouth again on a rough moan that would have normally shocked her, embarrassed her. But it didn't. And it wasn't because his kiss made things fuzzy—far from it. It was all sharper, more defined. Raw and real and all the better for it.

It was all instinct and feeling, lust and need. He was devouring her and she was willing, more than.

He slid his hand down and gripped her thigh, his fingers wrapping around at the sensitive spot behind her knee. He pulled up gently, opening her to him, wrapping her leg around his hip. It brought the blunt head of his arousal against the bundle of nerves at the apex of her thighs that was screaming for attentions, dying for satisfaction.

She rocked against him, following her instincts for once, leaving her head out of the equation.

This was about feeling. Not logic. Not duty. Not about pursuing worth.

She gave a slight growl of protest when he abandoned her mouth, and he laughed, pressing kisses to the side of her neck, her exposed collarbone.

"Zahir...oh, Zahir," she whispered, tightening her hold on his shoulders, her nails digging into his muscled body.

He froze, pulling his head away, the expression on his face dazed, clouded. And then clarity returned.

He pushed away from her, his chest heaving. "Enough."

"Zahir..."

"Why are you here, Katharine?"

"I...I wanted to read so I came down after dinner and..."

"No. Why are you here? In Hajar. With me."

"Because of Alexander. Because...because I need a husband to protect the throne of Austrich."

"If not for that, would you have come?"

She shook her head. "No." She spoke the word on a whisper, her entire body trembling."

He looked at her for a moment, his eyes bottomless wells

of ink. Flat and empty. Her stomach tightened in on itself, making her fight to keep upright.

He nodded curtly and turned and walked from the room, leaving her standing there, cold and more alone than she'd ever felt in her entire life.

# CHAPTER EIGHT

SHE wasn't used to saying the wrong thing. Or maybe she wasn't used to people showing their disapproval as openly. Unless of course it was from her father.

This, with Zahir, went way beyond disapproval, though. She'd hurt him. At least, she thought maybe she had. She wasn't certain that Zahir felt hurt anymore. She wasn't sure if there was anything behind that granite wall of his.

*Oh, no, there's...there's all that passion.*

Just for moment, she'd seen Zahir as he'd been. Effortlessly seductive, charming and sensual. As he had been? He still had it. He'd all but turned her to mush.

But that was just physical. A kind of physical she wasn't used to. But she knew enough to know that men didn't really need emotion to get into the physical. She wasn't entirely certain she needed it, either, considering how she'd responded to him.

Not that she was entirely void of emotion where he was concerned.

She thought back to that day in the market, his eyes like a hunted, wounded animal until she'd touched him. And when they'd cleared, in that moment, something had shifted in her. And it had only kept on shifting. The oasis. The dance. The kiss.

Nothing like the few chaste kisses she'd shared with Malik.

Theirs had been an attempt to find some passion between them, and she'd been certain that she could, but it hadn't been anything like being in Zahir's arms.

With him, she'd gone up in flames.

She still burned. She squirmed slightly in her reclining position on her plush bed, a slight sheen of sweat breaking out over her skin.

She could still feel the imprint of his hands on her, sliding over her curves, his tongue against hers. So sensual, in a way she hadn't imagined it could be. Her body felt overheated again, just like that. Just the thought of him.

Blinking hard, she turned her attention back to her tablet computer and swiped her fingers over the screen idly, flipping through a few more wedding gown designs. She wasn't certain it really mattered what she wore, but her usual dresser had sent her some amazing sketches, and it would be great publicity for him and the fashion designer who'd created them. So in that way, it sort of mattered.

She frowned. She was always doing that. Looking for the meaning in what she did. The weight. A way to make herself matter. She rolled over onto her stomach and pushed the tablet out of the way. She would just have Kevin pick one. Because she really didn't care. What did it matter anyway?

Zahir would rather not be having the wedding at all, and he wouldn't care if she walked down the aisle in clear tape and packing peanuts. So truly, the wedding gown was moot.

It didn't represent anything. A legal union that didn't go beyond the piece of paper they would both be signing. A different set of documents, another pair of signatures, and they'd be unmarried just as easily.

She'd leave the cake flavors and the canapés up to the wedding coordinator, too. Because it just didn't matter.

And it would matter even less if her groom couldn't stand there long enough for her to make it up the aisle. If a flashback hit him there and then and he was assaulted by the kind of fear she'd witnessed in his eyes before.

He'd been doing well. They hadn't taken a drive in a couple of days. Not since the kiss. But he had been doing well on them. His tension not as evident in his posture when they moved through crowded portions of the city.

*If not for that, would you have come?*

No.

The words repeated in her head over and over. Growing more and more acrid with each replaying. Of course, she'd had no other reason to come, but in that moment it had felt like a rejection to him.

It had been, but it had been to protect herself. Because she could so easily get lost in the kissing. In the passion and the desire, and forget that this was a temporary marriage. And that he wasn't able to feel emotion for her. That he would never want her in his bed night after night. That even if they gave in, the arrangement wouldn't last.

"I wouldn't want it to anyway," she said into the empty room.

She was headed to the light at the end of the tunnel. Except when she closed her eyes, she didn't really see a light anymore. She saw a man with bleak eyes and an obvious despair that seemed to reach deep into his soul.

"Katharine."

Zahir's deep, strong voice pulled her out of the fuzziness of her dreams and back into the stark reality of wakefulness. The afternoon sun was pouring through the window and spilling on the edge of her bed, where her hand was resting, steadily burning it to a bright pink.

She tugged it back and flexed her fingers. "Yes?" She turned to face him and her heart nearly stopped. He was just so powerful, his presence so full.

"Why is there an army of press at the door?"

"I don't…my father," she said, moving into a sitting position and scrubbing her hand over her face. "Such a good public showing, I'm sure, is important to him. A message sent to John. Letting him know that his hopes of gaining the throne are completely over."

She looked at Zahir, at the wild look in those dark eyes, and she felt a sharp stab of pain her stomach unlike anything she'd ever experienced. She wasn't helping here, that was for sure. She was dragging him into hell. For the sake of her own feelings of accomplishment?

No. This had been important. Real. John couldn't take the throne, and he couldn't be allowed to have influence over Alexander.

But the fact that Zahir had to get pushed into this…

She gritted her teeth. "We can tell them to go away."

She watched him, his shoulders straight, his eyes glittering in the light. He slowly curled his fingers in, the tendons on the backs of his hands standing out, showing the extreme pressure he was putting on them, on his body. "No," he said, his voice hard.

"Then we can ignore them." She could picture it. They could go out the back. Ride to the Oasis. The Oasis of Hope. It could be their refuge. It was tempting, very tempting to just ride away from everything. But in her mind, she was with Zahir, not away from him.

"No. We will go and make a statement." He flicked a dismissive glance over her. "Make yourself up, and meet me in the front corridor in twenty minutes."

Katharine was in the entryway two minutes early, her hair pinned up, wearing a bright yellow dress with a thick white belt that cinched the waist in. It was sunny. Chipper, even.

Maybe it would make her feel a little perkier. A little less like she was leading Zahir to the executioner.

Zahir walked in, clad in white linen pants and a sand-colored tunic that molded to his well-defined chest. He didn't go in for traditional dress, which didn't really surprise her. He wasn't the type to do something simply because it was what others had done before him.

His short dark hair looked like he'd simply combed it with his fingers. He hadn't tried too hard. In short, he looked like a man who didn't really want to be here.

But he'd come. And that was really what mattered. That was where the bravery was.

"Ready?" he asked.

"Yes?" she said, her voice hesitant.

"Better than that, Katharine."

"Yes. What exactly are we saying?"

"That we are getting married." He turned and walked back to the door, his posture straight, the injury in his leg giving his gait an uneven rhythm.

Her heart swelled in her chest, so big it was nearly painful. She felt his effort in her, felt the strength it took him to walk with his head held high.

She had never seen a bigger accomplishment than she saw in those few steps from her side to the door.

Two of his security staff pushed the doors open and flanked them on their way out into the courtyard. The press was behind the gate, their cameras aimed at Zahir. There was a rapid clicking of shutters and she saw the faintest twitch in the muscles of Zahir's face. But it was barely traceable. His expression remained mostly passive, his body stiff and straight.

"We don't have to do this," she said. "We can have a representative…"

"I will not walk away. I am not a coward, Katharine, whatever else I might be."

She nodded once and took three quick steps so that she was at his side.

"We will take three questions," Zahir said, standing in front of the massive, wrought-iron gate, his arms folded over his chest. The questions wouldn't matter, not to a media obsessed with seeing the Beast of Hajar, the man who had sequestered himself in the palace for so long, never having more than a blurred photograph taken of him since the attack that had shaken a nation.

"It's true? You're marrying Sheikh Malik's fiancée, Princess Katharine?" One of the reporters in the back shouted the question over the roar of voices.

"No. She is not my brother's fiancée. My brother is dead. I am marrying *my* fiancée." He barked the words, and she saw a group of sweat beads forming on his brow. She stepped closer, running her fingertips down his arm, the rough hair tickling her skin.

She felt him relax slightly beneath her touch.

"When is the wedding?"

"Just over a month away. One more."

"Princess Katharine! How is it to bed the Beast?"

His muscles locked beneath her hand. Anger burned in her stomach, threatened to boil over.

"I would not be so crass as to answer such a question," she said. She felt a slight tremor run through the hard muscle on his forearm. "But I will say this, it is a loss to women that I expect, and will receive, fidelity from my husband. A great loss indeed."

She felt some of the tension ease, at least she thought she did…somehow. She felt it in her, an echo of his own emotion and stress.

"That's all," he said, taking her hand in his and lacing his fingers through hers. She followed him back, away from the gate and back into the cool sanctuary of the palace. When the heavy doors closed behind them, Zahir lifted his hand and ran it through his hair.

His fingers shook as he did it, the one real crack in his strength she'd witnessed.

The security guards faded into the background, gracefully making their exit without ever betraying that they'd seen any weakness in their ruler.

That left Katharine and Zahir standing alone in the corridor. She searched for words. Something about the lack of class some people exhibited. Or maybe a few foul names to call the reporter who'd dared to ask that question. Or a few foul names for her father. For putting them in this position, for exposing Zahir to the scandal hungry European press.

He turned to her and her words dried on her tongue, along with all of the moisture in her throat. Dark emotion blazed in his eyes, a fire, a hunger, that made an answering, heated ache begin to burn in her stomach.

She backed up a step, and he advanced, one step, then two, and she didn't retreat again. He hooked an arm around her waist and pulled her to him, her breasts crushed against his hard chest.

His kiss was a shock, no preliminaries, no hesitation. He simply took. And she took back. She wrapped her arms around his neck, clinging to him as he clung to her. His hands were rough on her hips, gripping her firmly, his blunt fingertips digging into her flesh.

He backed her up against the wall, pressing her flat against the surface. She released her hold on him, turned her hands and pressed her palms against the cool inlaid gold and onyx, trying to find purchase, something to keep her from sliding to the floor. He released her mouth and curved his head, pressing hot kisses to her neck, down to her collarbone.

Zahir let go of her hips and moved his hand to hers. She wove her fingers through his, his weight keeping her pinned to the wall. But she didn't feel trapped or frightened. She was with Zahir. And she was protected.

She felt the tension ebbing from his body, flooding away as his passion mounted. But it was replaced with intensity of a different kind. An entirely new kind of need.

And she felt it, too. Her body ached for him, with need of him.

"Zahir," she whispered.

He went stiff in her arms, his intake of breath swift and harsh. And just like last time, he jerked away, his eyes clouded with desire. His erection was obvious, thick and ready, pressing against the filmy layer of fabric that concealed his body from hers.

He stepped back from her, his chest moving up and down sharply, his expression hard. "When you say my name," he said, his voice rough. "I come back to myself."

She didn't know why he said it that way, as though it pained him. She had used it in the alley, had been able to shake him from the flashback that had held him in its iron grip.

"I don't…"

"I do not want to come back to this body," he said, the words forced out of his throat. He turned and walked away, leaving her there, her arms still pressed against the wall as though he held her there.

Leaving her cold and hot and wanting more than she knew she would ever have.

Zahir wasn't a religious man. He never had been. Still, the habits of his people were ingrained in him, and drinking alcohol, especially to excess, had always been frowned upon by most in his culture. *He* had always frowned upon it.

He was tempted now. To drink everything away until it

all faded from him. To find something to numb reality, to make it less…real.

*No.* When reality faded, he lost time. He lost parts of himself. He saw that day. Had to watch it all play out from beginning to end.

*Ebn el sharmoota.*

He couldn't start down that path.

Instead, his thoughts turned to Katharine. He had been rough with her, worthy of his name. And yet she had given it all back to him. Her body so soft against his, soft but aggressive. Kissing her was anything but one-sided.

And she had been sweet. Five years without the touch of a woman. Without anything but the cold, clinical touch of doctors. But she was hot, her touch warm and so much more. Personal. It touched him beneath his skin, deep into him.

The attraction between them was electric. Beyond electric. It was a living thing, threatening to consume anything in its path.

And then she'd said his name. As she'd done that night in the study. As she'd done in the alleyway in the market. And it brought him back. Back from the abyss. Back from rapture.

Because he was Sheikh Zahir S'ad al Din, the Beast of Hajar. And she was the most beautiful woman he had ever seen in his thirty-three years. Everything about her was stunning perfection and he…

He was a monster. And it had little to do with his face.

Yet he lived. He lived in this shell of himself. No, he was not handicapped like he could have been. Limited vision and a limp were minor when compared to the fate of his family.

But he was not himself. He was hollow. He never moved on, and he never could. He felt nothing. Wanted nothing.

*No. That's not true.*

He wanted her. So much that the craving was nearly unbearable.

He tugged the tunic shirt off and discarded it, then stood, facing the bar. He could walk over there and get drunk. Wake up with a pounding headache and unsatisfied desire.

Or he could go and get the only thing he'd wanted in five long years.

Two things stopped him. Would she be with him out of pity? Be with him because she thought he'd changed the terms of the agreement? She was so determined for the marriage to go through he wouldn't be surprised. The other thing that stopped him was the fear of losing himself. When he kissed her, everything faded behind the red haze of passion. If he found release with her, if he allowed himself to be lost, he was not sure of what he might do.

He didn't know anymore, how much of him was the man, and how much was the beast.

He gritted his teeth. He might not be the man he had been, no, not even close. But he knew a woman's body. There were things he knew how to do very, very well. Tonight, he would give her every bit of that skill, pour all his desire into her needs.

And he would prove that he would not lose himself in the process. He would not be manipulated or used. He had the control, and he would show her.

Katharine flung the bedcovers back and stalked to the window. She was hot. And the desert wasn't to blame. The night air was cool and dry, and it was usually her favorite time in Hajar. But nothing could extinguish the flame that Zahir had lit inside her.

Nothing had been able to dampen it. The chilly shower she'd taken had only made her blood run nearer to the surface, had only made her more aware of all of the parts of her body. Tender, needy parts that wanted Zahir's rough, insistent hands on them. Without that sweet little yellow dress in the way.

She felt like her skin was too tight. Like she needed to shed it. At least shed her clothing. She arched against the silky camisole top she was wearing and the filmy fabric brushed over her nipples.

She sucked in a sharp breath. The slight abrasion of the fabric sent sensation arrowing down to the apex of her thighs, made inner muscles she had never been overly aware of tighten in response.

She took a handful of hair and twisted it around her hand, holding it up off her neck. It was damp with sweat and some of the coolness in the air finally made its way into her. Like the shower, it didn't help.

"Katharine."

She dropped her hair and let it fall down past her shoulders. Zahir was standing in the doorway, wearing nothing more than those pale linen pants, low on his narrow hips. Showing perfectly defined muscles, gorgeous bronzed skin.

He hid his imperfections in the shadows, and for a moment, it was easy to forget he had any. That made her feel strange. Like she was adrift in the sea without an anchor. Because without the scars—those marks that made him who he was—she didn't recognize him. It was only for a moment, but it was so strange and strong.

She moved nearer to him, breathed in a sharp breath when she saw the roughened side of his face.

"What are you doing here?"

"I am here to finish what should have been finished in the entryway today. What should have been finished last week in the study."

She drew in a shaky breath, just before his lips crashed down on hers. And then there was nothing beyond desperation. It clawed at her, tore at her stomach, creating a frenzied desire in her that seemed to possess her, drive her actions.

He slid his hand down to her backside, his palm resting on

the tiny silk sleep shorts she was wearing, his heat burning through the thin fabric. Even that was too much. The barrier was too inhibiting.

"I'm here to show you that there are still ways I can put any man to shame."

A tremor of desire spasmed in her and she wiggled against him. He locked his other arm around her waist, holding her still as he continued to kiss her, the strokes of his tongue slow and languorous against hers, then ferocious and hungry.

He moved his hand up, pushing her top up, making contact with her bare back. A short sound of pleasure escaped her lips.

"Good?" he asked against her mouth.

"Oh, yes."

He took both hands and moved them up her waist, his thumbs curving beneath her breasts, so close and so far, teasing her, tormenting her. She arched, begging him, needing him to give her more.

He chuckled, ignored her offering as he continue to move his hands over parts of her body that shouldn't have the power to send such erotic currents through her.

But they did. Her stomach, just below her belly button, to the top of the low waistband of her shorts, back up, thumbs skimming the plump flesh of her breasts without ever really touching them. Without ever satisfying the ache that burned within her.

He moved his hand to her back again, down so that both palms were flat on her backside. He pulled her into his body, let her feel the hard length of his erection pressing against her stomach. She rocked against him, seeking out any kind of satisfaction she could find, getting nothing but a tease.

And that only made her hotter, wetter, needier for more.

He knew it, too. He broke their kiss and looked at her, his eyes black in the dim light, his smile wicked, predatory. She was his prey, and he was clearly set on devouring her.

She shivered in anticipation. She had no problem with that scenario.

He lowered himself slowly, his lips soft on her neck, then the tip of tongue, gliding down between the valley of her breasts as his hands traveled upward, pushing her top up, his bare skin brushing her stomach, higher, to her breasts.

He went to his knees, pressed a hot kiss to her stomach. He fingered the edge of her camisole. "Assistance?"

She gripped the hem and pulled it up over her head, baring her upper body to him. She waited for embarrassment of some kind to hit, but it never did. She felt cocooned in the space, in the near darkness. It was their own place, and there simply wasn't room for embarrassment in it.

He pushed her shorts down to her ankles and she stepped out of them, kicking them aside. She was completely naked now, and it was fine. More than fine.

He moved his hands over her bare hips, thighs, around to her butt. "You are incredible." He pressed a kiss to her stomach again, tracing a line downward with the tip of his tongue. She moved her hands to his shoulders, holding on to him to keep from sinking into a puddle on the floor.

He teased her there, too. His tongue so close to the bundle of nerves that she knew was there just to send her over the edge into total, orgasmic bliss. He didn't, though, even though she had no doubt he could with the slightest flick of his talented tongue. He simply teased, his tongue moving over tender skin, making her body shiver with delight.

He stood suddenly, pausing to look at her, that wicked smile, the most genuine show of emotion beyond anger that she'd seen, was still on his face.

"The bed," he said.

And she knew it was an order. One she would gladly follow.

She walked backward, keeping her eyes locked with his,

until the backs of her knees hit the edge of the mattress. She sat down, pushed herself backward. It put her in a vulnerable position, like a buffet spread out for a starving man.

He joined her on the bed, his hands moving over her curves as he kissed her mouth with ravenous need.

He cupped her breasts, teased her nipples, sending sparks of pleasure skittering through her veins. He moved his other hand between her thighs, pushing two fingers near her entrance gathering the moisture there and sliding it over to her clitoris.

The slick stimulation was so good, everything she'd been waiting for. She didn't bother to suppress the groan of pleasure that climbed her throat.

He leaned toward her, flicked his tongue over nipple, then laved it with a long, broad stroke. "Oh, Zahir."

She paused then, afraid that she'd make him stop. Afraid she'd ruined it again.

A dark intensity lit his eyes and he dipped his head again, sucking the tip of her breast deep into his mouth, then running his tongue around the edge of her nipple.

"Say it again," he said roughly.

She never thought to do anything but comply. "Zahir."

"Again," he said, kissing her stomach, beneath her belly button.

"Zahir."

He parted her thighs with his broad shoulders, his grip on her legs keeping her immobile. Keeping her just where he wanted her.

He stroked her aching flesh, rubbing the tips of his fingers over her that most sensitive part of her again.

He lowered his head and followed the same path his fingers had just taken with the flat of his tongue. So hot and slick, so much more intense than anything that had come before. He explored her, pleasured her that way until she was certain she was going to have to shed her skin to find some relief from the tightening, spiraling sensation that made everything in her feel too large for her body.

He pushed one finger into her and stars exploded behind her eyelids, raining down on her, leaving little prickles of heat where they landed as wave after wave of pleasure moved in her, pulsing in time with her internal muscles.

She felt shell-shocked, numb and sensitized at the same time. Like it was too much and not enough.

Zahir moved up to lie beside her, caressing her face, stroking her hair, scattering kisses on her shoulder. His erection pressing hard and insistent against her hip.

"Now what?" she asked, making a move to cup his shaft.

He caught her hand in his, kissed her upturned palm. "More of the same."

He leaned in and kissed her mouth, and she started to melt again.

# CHAPTER NINE

WHEN the last shudder of pleasure escaped her lips, Zahir stood from the bed. Katharine rolled to her side and watched him. He was still half-dressed, and physically unsatisfied, his erection evident, pressing against his pants.

"Come here," she said, more than ready for that next step. He'd brought her to orgasm three times, and it was time, not just for his pleasure, but for her to have him. She didn't know why, but it felt possessive. Like he would belong to her when she had him inside of her.

"I think that's enough, don't you? Not that I haven't enjoyed watching you take your pleasure."

"Come and get some of your own," she said, not entirely understanding his cryptic statement.

"I've had plenty of it this evening. Tasting you, touching you, that was pleasure enough."

"Zahir..."

He turned away from her, the moonlight filtering through the window, catching the raised ridges of flesh that marred his back. "You are a virgin?"

"I...at this point only a technicality."

"You should remain that way then."

"Isn't that up to me?" she asked, clutching the bedcovers to her bare breasts and pushing herself into a sitting position.

"And me. If I do not wish..."

"You don't *wish* to be with me?" She looked down at the clear outline of his arousal. "I call foul on that."

"Tell me, is this virginity of yours a part of my marriage bargain?"

She felt heat creep into her cheeks. "More or less."

"Is that why you're still a virgin? Because you thought you might need it with Malik gone?"

"I… It's complicated. But I would be lying if I said that had nothing to do with it." It was shaming to admit. She'd never truly imagined any man would question it. Royals tended to have that view of the world. A virgin bride was important, and her being able to qualify as royal bride material had always been essential. A part of her purpose. The biggest part.

It had been ingrained in her that it was the right thing. That it was one of her commodities.

The thought made her sick now. It wasn't something she dwelled on, not usually. Why would she? She hadn't exactly had suitors banging down her door and part of her had been afraid that, if she'd chosen to seek out relationships, it would make her father start looking for someone else to sell her to.

She'd been enjoying her reprieve too much to let it end. But when marriage to Zahir had come up as her best option for protecting Austrich, she'd been ready.

"What if you need it later?" he asked, his tone dark.

"I'll be divorced," she said. "No one will expect it."

Her throat tightened. Was she really doing this? All but begging the man to have sex with her? Was she really thinking of sleeping with him now, divorcing him and finding someone else later?

Rage shook her, mingling with a slow, rolling shiver of shame that seemed to start in her stomach and move through her limbs, making her feel weak. Angry. "Get out."

He inclined his head. "As you wish, *latifa*."

He turned and walked out. She wanted to call him back. So she could scream at him. So she could make love with him.

She lay back down and curled her knees into her chest. She'd never felt so out of place in her own body. A body that was still humming from his touch, still lit up with pleasure, from all he had done. And inside...inside was raw. Tender and bleeding.

She thought back to the intensity she'd seen on his face when he'd first walked into the bedroom.

*I'm here to show you that there are still ways I can put any man to shame.*

He hadn't been here to prove it to her. He'd been proving it to himself. On the heels of the comment that journalist had made...and then Katharine had defended him. His pride had been on the line and he'd used her body to restore it.

He'd given her pleasure, more than she'd ever imagined possible, but it hadn't been hers. It had been his. His retribution. His proof.

She pounded her fist on her pillow and let out a growl of frustration. She had been his therapy yet again. She had proven useful.

Earlier today she might have accepted that. She'd been helpful, after all. Worthwhile. But that wasn't what tonight had been for her. It wasn't what she wanted it to be. She hadn't been out to prove her worth, she'd been in it for herself. For the driving need that made her body ache and her heart race.

But she didn't want to be his bandage. She'd wanted to be his woman. His lover.

And now she was just convinced that there was truly nothing behind the rock wall he'd built around his soul. Nothing but darkness.

Avoidance, it turned out, was easy in the Hajari palace, as long as it was what Katharine wished.

Zahir had hardly seen her in the week and a half since the impromptu press conference. Since he'd come to her room and tortured himself by inches while he tasted and caressed her gorgeous, smooth body.

All he had been able to do was worship her perfection. Because he had not allowed himself to take. He had been too afraid. Of what might happen. Of what he might do or say. Of harming her in some way. Of what might happen if the rock-hard barrier of his control burst and all of the images came pouring through while he was at his most vulnerable.

He had not allowed himself to seek women out. Had not allowed himself to remember the kind of oblivion sex could bring, because oblivion was not kind to him anymore. It made him lose everything. He could not do that to her. Lose himself in her. He would not be a man if he were willing to do such a thing.

He might harm her in the worst case scenario, and in the best, she would find herself without that bargaining chip she had in her virginity.

A shiver of disgust ran through him. He didn't see it that way, but his barbarian ancestors certainly had. His father, it seemed, had too. He doubted Malik had cared one way or the other. His brother had had such a laid-back manner, such an open acceptance and ease to him.

He was not Malik. That was for certain. Katharine would have been better off with Malik. Or with him, if the attack hadn't happened. An ache spread through him, fierce, painful. It was the first time he'd allowed himself to think of what might have been if he and Katharine had been able to meet before the attack. If they had simply been a man and a woman.

"But that isn't what happened," he said into the empty space of his office.

And all of his reasons for stopping himself from having sex with her remained.

But his body was punishing him for it. He woke hard and aching in the middle of the night, his mind filled with visions of her pleasure-clouded eyes, full, parted lips reddened from kissing. That soft, curvy body. Perfect in every way, nothing to mar to her luscious beauty. The sound of her soft sighs filling his ears.

It was better than images of exploding grenades and the sounds of chaos and screaming.

The door to his office opened and he knew it was Katharine. Anyone else would have knocked. Katharine didn't behave like everyone else. She didn't bow and scrape and defer to his every command.

"We leave for Austrich tomorrow."

"I'm aware of that."

"Well, I thought we should formulate a plan." She eyed him as though it was his fault there wasn't one, her pert chin angled out, her lips pursed.

He put his palms flat on his desk and stood, leaning in slightly. Her scent caught him, so warm and inviting. "I am not the one who has been doing the avoiding."

Her mouth opened and closed, reminiscent of a goldfish. "I have not been avoiding you."

"Well, you haven't invaded my bedroom or my gym in nearly two weeks, and it's been the same amount of time since you've invaded my office. Not only that, but you haven't taken Lilah out for a ride. You've been hiding."

"I don't hide," she said stiffly.

"Don't you?" He looked at her haughty pose, at those steely-green eyes of hers. "You're hiding now. Behind this facade. Emotionless, forceful, but I know the real woman. I've held her in my arms while she came apart with her pleasure."

Color flooded her pale cheeks. "Just because you gave me an orgasm doesn't mean you know me."

"That's not why I know you."

He didn't know why he said it, why he pressed. Except that he wanted her to admit that there was something between them. That there was heat. That she was more than the uppity princess that had stormed his castle over a month ago.

Because she was. He was certain of it.

*It should not matter. Whoever she is, she'll be gone when Alexander is of legal age. She'll never be yours.*

And he didn't want her to be. It was a cruel joke, the mere thought of it. Because she was perfection. She was light and open and beneath that spine of steel, there was strength.

He was darkness. And he wanted to remain in the shadows. How could he do anything else when no one else involved in the attack was able to do anything? They were gone. They could never move on from it. Why should he? How could he? It seemed his duty, his responsibility, to cling to the memory, but it kept him apart.

"Why do you know me then?" she asked, her full lips turned down into a frown.

"Because...you've given yourself to me."

It was true. She had. She was the image in his mind now, instead of grenades. When the crowd surrounded their town car in the market, he saw her face.

"I haven't given myself to you." She wrinkled her nose, as though the very idea disgusted her.

"I didn't seem so repellent to you the other night in your bed," he said, anger roaring through him immediately.

"That isn't what I mean! Obviously I don't... Obviously I...I don't belong to you."

"No, Katharine, you don't. You could never belong to any man. It is far too passive a place for you to be. And you are anything but passive."

"I don't know about that."

"I do. I have the internal battle scars to prove it. I simply meant you have taken time with me. Taken the time to try and…" He didn't like the word *help*. It seemed weak to him. And yet he'd needed it. And she had given it. "You have helped me."

She looked down. "I needed to."

His chest felt tight. "So that I can make a show of being a strong Regent to your country?"

She nodded, the motion jerky. "Of course." She looked up, her green eyes wells of emotion so deep he could not see the end of them. And he didn't want to. "Remember that it's much colder in Austrich than it is here. The air is thinner, too."

"Naturally."

"What time do we leave tomorrow?"

"If we leave in the morning we should arrive with daylight left in Austrich. Eight o'clock?"

She forced a smile. "I guess coordinating wasn't all that complicated."

Maybe it wasn't. But everything else was. Zahir wasn't the kind of man who did complicated. Everything in his life was simple. Get out of bed, get through the day, try to find some rest in the sleep that always tried to elude him.

Not since Katharine had come. And he could truly say he didn't want things back the way they were before she came.

But he wasn't sure he could stand six years of denying himself while she lived in the palace, as his wife. Untouchable and more tempting than any woman he had ever encountered.

Green trees, capped with pristine white snow blurred together as their private plane landed on the airstrip that was positioned behind the palace in Austrich's capital.

The deep saturation of color, after coming out of the washed-out landscape of Hajar was almost blinding in its intensity. Surreal as Katharine descended from the steps and onto the tarmac, her high-heeled shoe making contact with the icy ground.

It was never quiet in the desert. There was always the buzz of an insect or the sound of the wind skipping over the sand. But in Austrich, the mountains and trees offered insulation from noise, and brought a kind of silence that bordered on the surreal.

"You all right?" she asked, turning to face Zahir, who was looking at the sky, the gray, overcast sky that must seem completely foreign to him.

"Of course."

"You haven't…I mean, I know you and Malik went to school in Europe, but you haven't traveled outside of Hajar in…"

"Five years," he said, turning his focus to the craggy peaks that surrounded them.

"It's very different here. I remember the first time I went to Hajar I was in shock. I felt like I was right next to the sun."

He looked at her then, his dark eyes inscrutable. "You belong here."

"It's in my blood."

She knew he meant she didn't belong in Hajar. Didn't belong with him. As much as she knew it, she couldn't shake the feeling of foreignness that crept over her when she turned to face the castle, rising from the tall pine trees, towers gleaming in the faint glow of the sun.

This place, her home, it felt strange now. Stranger than it felt to be in Hajar.

"My father is expecting us." She turned and strode to the limo, waiting to drive them the thousand or so paces to the castle.

She allowed the chauffeur to open the door for her and before Zahir got in on his side she blew out a hard breath and fought with the urge to cry or scream or something. Something that would tear into Austrich's silence.

Something that would make her feel right.

She hadn't felt right since that night in her room. She wasn't entirely certain she'd felt right since the moment she'd walked into his office and proposed.

She closed her eyes. Had she even felt right before that? It had been a constant feeling, and she'd been used to it. But she wasn't certain it was the way she was supposed to feel. She was finding something else in Hajar, and she couldn't quite put a name to it.

The chill air from outside pierced the cocoon of warmth the limo offered, and Zahir slid inside beside her.

"Nice," she said, touching the dark sleeve of his wool jacket.

"I haven't had occasion to use it for quite a while."

"Not a lot of heavy coat weather in Hajar."

"No."

He turned his focus to the passing scenery and Katharine closed her eyes, trying to shut it all out.

Far too soon, the car slowed and stopped in front of the main entrance of the palace.

"How is your father doing?" Zahir asked.

"I don't know," she said, her voice choked. She hadn't seen him in over a month and he wasn't the kind of man who would admit to any frailty.

Their respective doors were opened for them in unison and they both stepped back out into the cold. Snow was falling now, sprinkling over the wide expanse of green lawn that dominated the palace courtyard.

There was no reticence in Zahir's demeanor, but then, her father wasn't a crowd. He strode ahead of her, his steps long and confident, and she tried to match them. Tried to feed off his strength, because for some reason, hers seemed to be failing.

She'd been treating Zahir like the enemy, because he'd hurt her, but she needed an ally now. Desperately.

The castle in Austrich was completely unlike the palace in Hajar. There were domestic staff everywhere, administrative personnel, visiting members of parliament and the occasional tour group. It was always busy, and it was never empty.

There were always flowers. And the most awful, gaudy garlands made of fresh vines and carnations strung over the public portions of the palace. High-gloss white marble floors and bright white, spotless walls with the matte impression of *fleur de lis* impressed upon them.

It felt foreign now, too, like the whole setting of the country had when she'd first stepped onto the tarmac. She moved a little bit closer to Zahir.

"This way," she said, indicating which direction her father's office was in. He would be there, waiting to greet her. Anything else would be far too casual. And anyway, this was a matter of State. Her wedding was about alliances and protection. Nothing more.

It would do her well to remember that.

They stopped in front of the heavy, dark walnut door that stood out in sharp contrast to the white walls, and Katharine took a deep breath, one she'd hoped would fortify her. It didn't.

"Katharine." Zahir touched her hand. "Look at me."

She looked up into his eyes, at his handsome face.

*You bring me back to myself.*

That was how she felt, like he'd brought her back to herself. She took another breath, and this time, she did feel fortified.

"If you can storm my office like you did, you can certainly do this."

She nodded and cleared her throat, knocking on the door with as much authority as she could muster. He was right. She had stormed his office. And then she'd moved in. She could do this.

"Yes?" Her father's voice sounded thin coming through

the door and it made her heart tighten. Because in so many ways she'd never truly thought of him as being human, mortal. But he was.

She pushed the door open and walked in. His office had always been different from the rest of the palace. Expansive, like everything else, but dark. Plush, navy blue carpets and dark wood paneling. He probably thought it gave it weight. It worked.

"Father, I would like to present Sheikh Zahir S'ad al Din, my future husband."

Her father stood, and she noticed how shrunken his frame had become, how much more gray was streaked through his hair. "Sheikh Zahir, I am glad you decided to honor the agreement. Your family was always trusted by mine."

It didn't escape Katharine's notice that it was Zahir her father addressed, not her.

Zahir nodded. "Katharine put forth a convincing argument."

Her father arched an eyebrow. "Did she?"

Katharine gritted her teeth, fought against the burning feeling of…of injustice that was rolling through her. It was as though she wasn't in the room. And now wasn't the time to be angry with her father. Not when he was sick like he was. It wasn't the time to see, so clearly, just how unimportant she truly was.

"She did. I said no, in fact, but she put forth some very good points." Zahir looked at her, deferring to her. Her father looked even more surprised by that.

"It's true," she said, clearing her throat. And then she was lost for words, unable to find a way to say that she'd been brave or made good points in favor of the marriage. She just felt small. Insignificant. Everything she'd always feared she truly was.

Her father looked back at Zahir. "I can well imagine what might have convinced you."

Bile rose in Katharine's throat. "Excuse me, please, I need to… It was good to see you, Father." She turned and walked out of the office, striding down the hall without pausing until she reached a segment of corridor that she knew was most likely to be vacant.

She leaned against the wall and took a breath, trying to undo the knot of pain that had gripped her heart.

How had she never realized? How had she never truly known just how little her father thought of her? She'd known he didn't think she was capable of ruling, that he'd imagined her less because she was a woman. But she hadn't realized that the quiet, insidious voice that whispered in her ear, told her how dangerously close she was to total insignificance, had been his voice. That it had been hidden, layered in every word he spoke.

Today it had been clear.

She heard heavy footsteps and she pushed away from the wall, schooling her face into a stoic expression. Zahir came around the corner, his left hand pressed against the wall, his jaw tight.

"I told him never to speak to you, or about you, that way again. Why didn't you tell me, Katharine?"

"Tell you what?"

"What a raging bastard the man is."

"I didn't…I didn't really realize. Until he started insinuating that I used my…body…to talk you into marriage."

"You could walk away, you know." His dark eyes were intent on hers, and for a moment, she wanted to take him up on that. To take his hand and walk out. Walk away.

"I'm not doing this for him. I'm doing it for Alexander. For my people. But I'm not going to worry about proving myself by doing it. Not anymore." She bit her lip and shook her head. "I wanted him to see that I was...that I could be just as important. But he never will."

"It's different with the heirs. They need confidence. They need to understand the weight of their duties. They need to be prepared to lead. The spares like us...we are incidentals."

"Were you?"

He looked behind her. "My parents were good to me. When I saw them. Malik was my father's priority, and that is understandable in a sense."

"But *you're* the one ruling Hajar."

He swallowed. "Yes. And you're the one saving Austrich."

She smiled at him, the motion a near impossibility. "When I have children, I won't rank them like that. I refuse to do it."

"I'll never have children, so that isn't an issue."

"Never?"

"They would cry at the sight of me."

"They would love you."

The light in his eyes changed, a strange, deep sort of longing opening up behind it. It reached into her soul, tugged at her heart. In an instant, it was gone, his control returned. "I would not know how to love them."

The bleak pain in his eyes nearly broke her. "You could, Zahir. You would."

"You don't know what it's like in here." He tapped his chest. "Empty. Thank God."

"Because feeling hurts too much?"

"There's hurt, and then there's the feeling that your insides are being ripped into pieces and scattered throughout your body. Left to bleed, stay raw and blindingly painful forever. At some point...you become dead to it. And to everything else. Good and bad. But anything is better than that kind of pain."

Her heart felt like it was tearing, mirroring what he had described. She put her hand on her chest. "But you still have pain. It finds you still. I've seen it. Why deny yourself good things, Zahir?"

"How can I accept all the things in life, my family, our guards, the innocent bystanders who were simply caught in the crossfire, will never have a chance to have." His eyes were flat again, the connection lost.

He turned like he was going to leave, and she blurted out a question to keep him there. "So, what did my father say when you told him off?"

"Nothing. He is, perhaps, still in there choking on his ire. But he will not push. He needs me, remember?"

"He's really not bad, Zahir. He has old, set ideas and tunnel vision ambition. He's done wonderful things for the country. As a ruler, he's a man of great compassion. As a father... not quite so much. But I respect all that he's done here, and I support him in that wholly."

"And I'm still going to help ensure that Austrich is protected."

She couldn't help but realize that he'd only named her country, and not his. That his priorities seemed to have shifted. People and not trade, right and not money.

But she suspected that truly, that had been in him from the beginning. He simply hadn't been willing to reach in and find it.

Now he had.

# CHAPTER TEN

THE snow relented for the day of the wedding, the sun shining down on the glistening blanket of white that covered the entire grounds of the castle.

Katharine adjusted her grip on her bouquet of pale, pink roses and closed her eyes, banishing the butterflies that were swirling around in her stomach.

It had been a long, hectic couple of weeks with Zahir and her father hashing out details, and Alexander sitting in on the meetings, trying to understand his place in a man's world when he was little more than a boy.

She knew sixteen wasn't really a child, and that a hundred years ago, he would have been placed straight on the throne. But he seemed so young. Much too young. It made her grateful for Zahir all over again.

The wedding, though, still terrified her.

She hadn't seen Zahir in twenty-four hours and she didn't know how he was feeling about it. About standing before a massive crowd of people. If his muscles were bound up by tension, as she'd witnessed on drives into town. If he would get lost in another flashback.

Suzette, her one bridesmaid, lifted the train of her dress and dropped it gently, letting the air catch hold of it so that it fanned over the ground, the sun shining through the window of the cathedral catching the delicate lace, the rays shining through the gossamer fabric.

"Totally gorgeous, Kat," she said.

Katharine sighed.

It was perfect. Perfect on the surface, at least.

*And that's all that matters.*

She turned to Suzette, the only person she could really count as a close friend. The American heiress had gone to the same boarding school Katharine had and they'd forged a bond. It was a bond that had loosened since adulthood, but if she ever needed anything, the chipper blonde was always willing to drop whatever she was doing and make sure she was there for her. And Katharine had always done the same for her.

"Suzette, is Zahir in there?" she asked, gesturing to the sanctuary, hoping the other woman had seen him at some point.

"I don't see why he wouldn't be," she said, straightening the top on her pale green gown.

Katharine sighed. "You're right. Of course. Prebridal nerves."

Suzette's eyes widened. "Not wedding night nerves, I hope. Because if so…we need to have a talk after the ceremony."

Katharine huffed a laugh, her face heating as she recalled her night with Zahir. The way he'd made her feel, the decadent things he'd done. Yes, she was still a virgin on technicality, but from the cold comments she'd heard some women make about sex and past lovers, she had a feeling she had a better grasp on what was meant to pass between a man and a woman than some with ten times her experience.

"Not that," Katharine said. "Not in the least." Although, now that Suzette mentioned it, she wondered if it being their wedding night would mean anything to Zahir. If he would want…

No. Likely not. He'd basically said he had no desire to sleep with her, a statement she didn't believe. But there was something behind it, she couldn't deny that.

"Just, actual vow-taking nerves," Katharine said. And nerves about whether or not her groom would do well beneath the pressure, with all those people crowded near him.

She pictured him, walking tall out of the palace of Hajar, going to meet the reporters at the gate. He was strong, her Zahir.

*My Zahir?* Yes. He sort of did feel like hers. Like a part of her. She couldn't explain it, and she didn't really want to. She didn't really want it to be true, either. Because that part of herself would have to be surgically removed when they parted in a few years' time. And if it was this bad now…

So much for calming her nerves.

"Just a sec." Suzette walked in front of her and opened the heavy wooden door that led into the sanctuary, just enough to see in. She turned to face her and offered a wide smile and a thumbs-up.

Katharine offered a weak smile back, her stomach dropping into her toes when the music suddenly changed. It was showtime.

Zahir's fingertips felt cold, and he knew it wasn't due to the snow outside. The slow onset of panic was distinct. His heart rate increased, his muscles tightened, his stomach clamping down like a steel trap. And his fingers always grew numb. He didn't know why. He only knew it was far too familiar a feeling for his liking.

It was a small wedding, by royal standards, at Katharine's request. That had been out of deference to his issues, he was certain. Something that galled.

Still, small meant at least two hundred guests, filling the

ancient stone sanctuary, along with the music of the strong quartet. It was loud. Packed. He could feel it all closing in.

A curvy little blonde in a spring-green dress began her walk down the aisle. She was Katharine's maid of honor; he nearly remembered being introduced to her the night before, although now, her name escaped him. It had all become very fuzzy. Everything seemed a little fuzzy.

He blinked hard, tried to ignore the metallic tang that coated his tongue. The fear that seemed to be slowly binding his muscle and sinew, making him feel frozen, stiff.

He was not a man given to prayer. But standing there, in a church, he felt it appropriate to send up a request. That he not do this here. He had wanted to do it all on his own strength, and yet it was proving impossible. He would take borrowed strength if he could use it to simply get through.

The sharp change in the music cut through the fuzzy edges of his mind, and he turned his focus to the doors that led from the sanctuary out into the foyer. They parted, and all of his focus zeroed in on the angel that moved through them.

An answer to his prayer.

Katharine looked as though she was floating, her strawberry-blond hair cascading over her shoulders, the frothy, lacy dress flowing and shimmering with each step she took. But that wasn't what held him captive.

It was her face. The same face that had brought him back in the marketplace. The same face he had watched alter beautifully as he gave her pleasure.

As Katharine came into view everything else faded away. It was as they had planned it, of course. But he had not imagined it would work quite so well.

He extended his hand, and she took it, and in an instant, he was warm again.

He leaned in. "You didn't have your father give you away."

She shook her head. "This was my decision," she whispered.

Good for her. Katharine was running on extra strength today, too, it seemed.

The priest spoke in Latin, and at length. And Zahir didn't know the meaning of the entire ceremony. But he did know what the bejeweled goblets filled with sand placed near the back of the stage meant. A Hajari tradition, one that he had not thought would be included here.

The vows were spoken in each of their native languages, and before the priest made his pronouncement, he gestured to the two chalices of sand. One filled with white sand, one golden brown, set on either side of a clear glass vase.

"Now Sheikh Zahir and Princess Katharine have chosen to seal their vows with a tradition from the Sheikh's homeland," he said, his voice thinner in English, his tone disdainful.

"What is this?" Katharine whispered.

"A Hajari tradition. Your father must have seen fit to add this." Because he'd known what it meant. An unsubtle reminder, perhaps, that the union was meant to be permanent.

Keeping her hand in his, he led her to the table, where they knelt on velvet cushions.

"What does it mean?" she asked, keeping her voice hushed.

He picked up both cups, and handed the one filled with white sand to Katharine. "The sand represents us, as individuals. Today, we do not leave here as two, but one."

He tipped his cup over the vase and poured a measured amount inside it. "Now you," he said.

Katharine did the same, and then he repeated the motion until they had emptied the cups, layering the sand into the vase.

"You are still there," he said, pointing to a bright streak of sand. "As am I. But, just like the sand, we will be impossible to separate. We are bonded together."

Katharine's green eyes looked glassy, her mouth dropped in shock. He leaned in and put his lips near her ear. "I'm sorry. I did not know this would be a part of the service."

She nodded stiffly. "It's…it's all right."

He led her back over to where the priest stood, her hand trembling in his. The priest made his pronouncement, and gave the command to kiss the bride. A command Zahir was more than happy to follow. Just for another taste, brief though it would be.

He leaned in slowly, watched her green eyes flutter closed as he descended. He pressed a soft kiss against plump, tender lips. The sensation was enough to take him out at the knees. Explosive in every way. Incredible.

And it was only a hint of the kind of pleasure her body offered. He knew, because he'd experienced much deeper torture at her hands. Rather, his own. She had been ready. And he had been forced to deny them both.

She pressed her mouth more firmly against his and he simply rested there for a moment, caught up in her touch. Just a moment of warmth. Of being surrounded by her.

Then he pulled away, his hand still joined with hers and the guests clapped for them as the priest introduced them as a married couple for the first time. He thought he felt Katharine's fingers tighten on his, almost imperceptibly.

They walked down the aisle together, the crowd a blur as they passed by. And he kept his eyes on Katharine, and his mind firmly in the present.

"Ready?" Zahir asked, his hand extended.

The crowd had made a half circle in the massive ballroom, preparing for the bride and groom dance.

The reception had been a blur from the moment they'd walked in, so many well-wishers, and cake, and a fountain that was spraying punch. It was everything a wedding should be. Except real.

The sand had thrown her. It had been so symbolic, the depth of it a shock she hadn't anticipated. It was how marriage should be. Their own color, their own individuality still on show, yet entwined with their partner's. There would be no easy way to separate the sand, and it had struck her then, how hard it would be to separate herself from Zahir.

But she would have to. As long as she remembered that she would be fine. She just couldn't forget. The sand was just a thing. Just sand. It wasn't them.

But in that moment...

"Yes, I'm ready."

They moved into the open area that had been cleared for the dance, and Zahir drew her into his body, one arm banded across her waist.

They had a live orchestra this time instead of the slow, sensual music they'd danced to in the library at the palace. But the guitar music was what she heard in her head. She felt everything recede.

Oh, so dangerous. So stupid. And yet, she found she couldn't fight it. Didn't want to.

He leaned in, his cheek pressed against hers, the skin rough on hers. But it felt right. It felt like Zahir.

"We made it through," he said, his voice soft, his breath hot against her neck.

"You did it," she whispered.

"I looked at you."

They didn't speak again, they simply moved with the music while Katharine fought the overwhelming tide of emotion threatening to consume her.

She could feel his heart beating against hers, matching hers. She'd never felt so close to anyone before. Had never wanted so badly to hold someone to her. And she didn't want to know what that meant.

So she just wouldn't think. Not now.

When the song ended, Zahir released her. It happened far too soon. If it were possible to freeze a moment, she would have done it with that one. In that moment, the desire to be in his arms was simple. She had accomplished what she'd needed to accomplish as far as the marriage went and she could rest. And be happy for a moment.

"I need a drink," she said, as they walked back off the floor. "You?"

"I am ready to be done." The way he said it, the look in his dark eyes…she wondered if he wanted to claim his wedding night. In the most traditional sense of the word.

Her pulse pounded, her blood turning fizzy in her veins. And if he did? If he did, she didn't think she'd refuse him. Quite the opposite. He was in her already, mingled in who she was, like the grains of sand in the vase.

"Just…just a moment." She turned and headed to the punch table, giving a finger wave to a cluster of women she'd gone to school with.

"Katharine?" One of the women, Katharine couldn't remember her name, stepped to the forefront of the group. "You aren't going to live in Hajar now, are you?"

Katharine frowned. "Of course I am. We'll still be here sometimes, of course." Especially if Zahir had to fulfill his duties as Regent. Most of it could be done remotely, especially with parliament in the solid shape it was in. But there would be traveling.

The other woman narrowed her eyes. "Won't you have to wear a veil there?"

Katharine shook her head. "No. Women aren't veiled in Hajar."

One of the women in the back, Ann, Katharine remembered, because she'd always been awful, snorted a laugh. "It's not the *women* who need to be veiled, though, is it?"

Katharine stiffened, anger rolling through her. Anger and the need to strike out, to wound as she was wounded. Because the comment seemed aimed at her heart.

Everything in her itched to slap the smug smile from the other woman's face. But with press everywhere, it would be the slap heard around Europe. And while part of her found that very attractive, she knew it would end up being much more trouble than it was worth.

"If that's your assessment it's clear you don't know what true sex appeal is, Ann," she said, keeping her voice as soft and even in tone as possible. "And my husband has it."

"In that case," Ann returned, "you had better hope you have it in you to hold on to him. I remember how you were in school. Trust me, sweetheart, rule following isn't sexy. And a shy little virgin like yourself, and no point pretending you aren't, is hardly going to hold the interest of a man who's done so much…living."

A sharp slug of anger and insecurity jabbed at her. She knew Ann was just taking strips off her because it was what Ann did, but that didn't erase the small amount of damage her remarks had done. It didn't help that Zahir didn't seem to have too hard a time resisting her. That he'd been in bed with her, toying with her body, bringing her past the point of reason and control, and then simply walked away hadn't been the biggest ego boost anyway.

Ann's eyes widened and Katharine turned sharply, into the warmth of Zahir's solid chest. His fingers curled into her arms, pulling her more tightly against him, the strength in his touch reminiscent of the day in the market.

She looked into his eyes, black wells of anger, and she knew he was still with her. But he was not happy.

And judging by the wide-eyed fear registering on Ann's face, she knew it.

"If you have upset my bride, I will have no choice but to see you out. And I will not bother to send for the guards," he said, his voice hard.

"It's fine, Zahir," Katharine said, unaccustomed to having someone stand up for her. It touched her, though, made her feel warm. Drew out the venom from Ann's insult.

"Ready, *latifa*?" he asked, the darkness radiating from him in palpable waves.

"More than," she said, caressing his arm lightly before following him out of the knot of people.

When the guests noticed they were leaving, there was major fanfare, and they lined the sides of the ballroom, flinging white petals onto the marble floors. A pathway for the bride and groom, a symbol of new beginnings.

As they made their way out of the massive room she felt Zahir tensing beside her, felt the burning heat of his rage as it warmed his skin.

When the heavy doors closed behind them, Zahir ran his hands over his short dark hair and stood still for a moment, not looking at her, before he turned and stormed out the door that led into the gardens.

Katharine lifted the skirt of her dress so the hem didn't drag on the ground and followed him out into the dark, crisp night. "Zahir?" His name came out with a cloud of condensation.

"Go, Katharine. Get changed. Rest."

"What's going on?"

He whirled around, his shoes crunching on the frozen snow, his top lip curled into a sneer, the expression tugging at his scars, exaggerating them.

"Is it what Ann said about…you?" she asked.

"Is that what you, think, Katharine? That I am so vain she managed to wound my pride?"

"It wounded me," she said.

"Why? I don't care what she thinks. But I didn't like the way she made you look…she…hurt you."

"She did. I didn't like what she said about you. Or me."

"I almost lost it, Katharine. For all of my tightly held control today, that almost did it. It reminded me of something Amarah said. That no matter how well my injuries healed, I would never be the man I was before. She was right. No matter how hard I try, it doesn't change anything. Not really." He turned away from her again and she knew that they were done with the conversation.

"It does. A month ago you couldn't have walked into that room without being thrown into a flashback. That's change, Zahir."

"It isn't real. It doesn't change the fact that I could still lose my control at any time. At any moment. And that is like knowing I could descend into hell. At any time. At any moment. Go to bed." He turned away from her, his broad back filling her vision.

She wanted to reach out to him, to touch him, and yet she knew he wouldn't welcome it.

"I'll be in our room," she said tightly. Her things had been moved into his suite for the wedding night, and of course there was no way either of them could have opposed it, not when the public was supposed to believe it a real marriage. And her father was meant to believe it was permanent.

She walked back inside and wandered through the empty corridors, up the winding staircase that led to the suite Zahir had been installed in when he'd first arrived. She pushed open the door and kicked her high heels off, the arches of her feet burning when she was finally standing flat-footed on the ground.

She sat down on the edge of the bed, the thick fabric of the wedding gown bunching up around her hips. Zahir. Her heart ached for him. Her heart ached for herself. And she wanted to punch stupid Ann in the face. Because he had done well. So well. And it wasn't fair.

She rested her chin on her palms. She shouldn't even stay in here. No one would know if she went back to her room. She grimaced. Yes. The staff would know. And while they were certainly not bad people, if offered the right incentive, secrets might get spilled. She flopped back onto the bed, her dress spread around her. The time difference, the wedding, the entirety of the last month and a half…it all caught up with her.

The world felt as though it tilted and she closed her eyes. Then she was falling through the mattress, sinking into a sleep brought on by exhaustion and grief.

Zahir walked into the bedroom, his fingers stiff from the cold. His knee was nearly frozen and the pain was blinding. Likely a little bit of arthritis, brought on by the injury, made worse by the cold weather. Something to make him thankful for the melting heat of Hajar.

He prayed again that he would never have to spend too much time in this freezing iceberg of a country.

His eyes caught hold of a bright white shape on the bed, glowing in the darkened room. Katharine, spread out like a snow angel in her lacy bridal gown. His chest constricted and he battled to take in a breath.

Hearing her in the position of defending had been…in all the low points in his life, it had ranked. And considering the lows he'd endured, that was saying something.

But he was her husband. He was meant to protect her. Even if he was only a temporary husband. And when he'd gone to do that, when the woman had turned her insults to Katharine…he had been nearly frozen. For fear of the swelling emotion in his chest giving way to something beyond him, bigger than him. It had been rage, and a kind of fierce protectiveness he'd only ever experienced during that flashback in the market.

Of course, Katharine wasn't the kind of woman who would ask for protection. She was the kind of woman who stormed a castle and claimed her future husband, not caring if he had a reputation as a monster.

His impression of her in the ballroom had been that she was a tigress. And that held true. Even if she did look delicate now.

"Now that she's retracted her claws," he mumbled to himself, loosening his tie and sitting in the chair that was next to the bed.

He didn't imagine sleeping in a gown like that—the kind that had to have layers of fabric and boning and whatever other medieval torture device women were using to attempt perfection these days—was comfortable, but he didn't dare help her out of it.

Because, while the dress was lovely, it was without the gown that Katharine was perfection. And if he touched her soft skin, just a brush of her bare body against his palm, he would be lost.

It would be easy now. To wake her with a kiss, to take advantage of the dark, and her sleepiness. He ached to. Shook with his desire. But he was poised on the brink, balancing on the edge of a blade. His control was ready to snap. The feelings she roused in him were unknowable to him. For so long, he had simply been dead. Feeling again…he did not know what to do with it. What it might do to him.

Or to her. Katharine was everything lovely and light.

He feared that the darkness in him would consume that.

# CHAPTER ELEVEN

SOMEONE was yelling. A terrified sound. Terrified, but full of rage.

Zahir opened his eyes and realized it was coming from him. He braced himself on the arms of the chair, his breath coming in short, powerful bursts.

A cool hand pressed against his forehead and the darkened room started to come into some focus.

"Are you all right?"

It was Katharine. Again tonight he was a fool in front of her.

He tightened his hands into fists and stood from the chair. Katharine stepped out of his way. He couldn't see her expression in the dark. But he didn't want her to see his, either, so that eliminated the possibility of turning on any lights.

"Fine," he gritted. Anger erupted from him, his body unable to contain any more tension. He had reached the end of it. "At least it didn't happen today, right? At least I didn't shame you with it. Though I came close."

She stood there, arms crossed, her head cocked to the side. He still couldn't read her face.

"What do you dream about, Zahir?"

Why not tell her? Why hold it back? She had seen it all. She had seen him flashback, and now she had seen him in the grips of the terror that sometimes found him in his sleep. There was no more pride left to lose.

"People. And then there is screaming, and darkness and nothing. It's the nothing that terrifies me the most," he said, closing his eyes. Instead of the scene he had described, he saw Katharine as she had looked coming down the aisle, an angel. His bride. "It was like…not existing. For endless hours. Or maybe it was only seconds. But it was a void. Cut off from everything, even pain. I fear sometimes, it wants to pull me back in."

She knelt before him, clasping her hands on his. "It won't. It can't."

He opened his eyes again, and she was still there, her face in his mind, and before him.

"I'm always afraid that I missed something," he said, his voice hoarse. "If I had only been paying attention more that day. I could have stopped it. It eats at me. And I always have to watch. It makes the flashbacks, the lost time, feel even more dangerous. And how is that for honesty?" he gritted.

"I don't think less of you for being affected, Zahir. I would wonder what was wrong with you if you weren't."

"Why do I live, Katharine, when everyone else…when they do not? It is the thing I cannot seem to reconcile."

She took a step closer to him. "For some reason, you seem to assume that you are less worthy. You aren't."

"You say it with such confidence."

"Because I know you."

"I have wondered—" he swallowed "—if it was a mistake."

"It won't be if you don't make it one," she said. "Look at all you've done for Hajar. You've made the economy, your people, stronger. And you've helped mine."

"It is the voice in my head. You know what I mean. Your father, he's the voice in yours."

"We need new ones."

"No argument."

She went back to the bed and climbed onto the left side, lying on her stomach, her arm under her face. He went to the right side of the bed and lay on his side, looking at the shape of her body, outlined in the pale moonlight.

Sleep tugged at him again, and he went. And his mind was filled with Katharine.


Katharine had never imagined that being back in the heat of Hajar could be a relief. And yet it was. Austrich was her home in many ways, and yet, in just as many ways it wasn't. There was a disconnect there. A kind of stress unique to being in the same space as her father.

She was free of that here. At least more so than she was back at the palace.

She wondered where Zahir was free. If he ever was.

He'd just lain next to her last night. On their wedding night. Never making a move to touch her. She'd wanted him to. She'd hoped he would.

She didn't know to what end. No, she knew, the end would be heartbreak for her. Because if she got any closer to him... it would be impossible to be away from him.

In him, she saw the definition of strength. It didn't mean never showing a crack, it didn't mean not feeling fear or despair. It meant going on anyway. As he did.

"Do I have...what am I meant do now?" she asked as they walked into the Hajari palace.

"Here?"

"Yes."

"Go on as you always have. Without moving any furniture, of course."

He spoke the words with humor and it made her stomach tighten. That something that had been so devastating to them didn't have that kind of power over him anymore.

"No, of course not."

"You could, actually," he said, his voice deadpan.

"I could what?"

"Move furniture if you want to. Just make sure I know. But you're right, Katharine, this is your home now. And that means you should be allowed to live in it. You aren't a captive, and this isn't prison."

"Thank you," she said, her throat tightening.

He looked at her for a moment, a muscle ticking in his jaw. He raised his hand, cupped her cheek, stroking his thumb over her skin. And he simply looked at her. He didn't lean in for a kiss, like she hoped he would. He simply stared, his touch soft, intoxicating. And so not enough.

She raised her hand and covered his with it, holding him to her, just for a moment.

Emotion filled her, overflowed and threatened to spill out. Emotion she didn't want to feel. Emotion she shouldn't feel. But she did. And she didn't want to identify it. Even if it was standing in her subconscious waving a name tag in her face, letting her know just what it was. What it had to be.

She had to ignore it. Because if she didn't...

Zahir said he didn't feel love. But he felt pleasure. She knew he did. She had felt his body, hard against hers, and she knew what it meant. Knew that he wanted her as she wanted him.

Because as stupid as it would be, and she had well and truly established that it would be stupid, she wanted to know what it was like to be with Zahir.

Selfishly, she wanted more of what he'd given to her that night in her room. That rolling, building pleasure that broke like a wave over rocks and left her spent and breathless in the aftermath.

But that wasn't all. She wanted to give to him, too. She

wanted him to understand that, no matter who he was before, he was the man she wanted. The man he was now.

She moved away from him out of necessity, because if he kept touching her like that, she was going to do something bold. And she was saving her bold for later. For the plan that was formulating.

"I might go out walking later. I was thinking I might go to the Oasis."

"If you wish." He frowned. "I do not want you to go alone."

Neither did she. "Can you come with me?"

"After I'm through in my office. Some things backed up while I was gone."

"More papers to sign? Sorry."

The corner of his mouth lifted. "It's all right. You were right. If I'm here, I have to make sure it matters that I'm here. I may not be a soldier anymore, not in the way I was, but I am still here to protect my country. My people. To stand in the gap for them, even if that takes the form of sitting behind a desk approving legislation."

"Go for it," she said, her heart suddenly feeling too big for her chest.

"I'll see you later."

Yes, he would. And she had plans for him. Big, important plans. The kind that made her feel shivery all over, and completely weak in the knees.

Zahir watched the sway of Katharine's hips as she walked in front of him, her body barely covered by another of her tempting sundresses. The pack she'd decided to bring was bounding in time with her steps, and for some reason, it drew his attention even more insistently to her pert, round butt.

Of course, that could be because he was a man, and, no matter what, that's where his attention was inclined to go.

Yes, he was only a man, one who had gone entirely too long without sex, and she tested him beyond his limits.

Out here, in the desert, he could take her. Make her his.

The need, the desire to do it was so strong he was nearly immobilized by it.

He could not. Even with only the desert bearing witness, it wouldn't change the risk. It wouldn't change the fact that he would be using her.

"I might need some help," she said, gesturing to the large stones that helped keep the Oasis closed off from the rest of the desert.

He raised an eyebrow and walked over to where she was. She smiled at him, a little bit too widely, and a little bit too innocently for his taste. "Help?" he asked, not believing her at all.

She nodded. "Just a little bit. Just help…um…help me keep my balance."

She stepped up into the rock, her range of motion limited by the skirt of her dress, and he put his hands on her waist, ensuring she didn't fall backward, although he highly doubted she would have.

Still, it was worth it. Touching her again, feeling her soft body beneath his hands…he had nearly lost it in the palace earlier when he'd touched her cheek. He'd been so tempted to lean and brush her lips with his, then press her body against the wall as he'd done earlier.

To spend all of his passion in her, to give her pleasure like she'd never known. Oh, yes, that was what he wanted.

He ignored the pressure of his growing erection as he climbed the rock after her and stepped into the shelter of the Oasis. The sound of running water reverberated off the rock walls, the chill it provided so welcome in the heat of the desert.

Katharine set her pack down and reached her arm around

behind her, doing what could only be described as a shimmy before the shoulder straps on her dress loosened and drooped.

"What are you doing?"

"I thought we might swim," she said. Again, far too innocent.

"There is a pool in my gym."

"I know." She shrugged her shoulders and the dress melted into a puddle of fabric at her feet.

She was left standing in nothing but a pale yellow bikini that barely covered her curves. And it was still too much. She bent and opened the zipper on her backpack and straightened again, the expression on her face guilty. "I brought you some shorts." She held out the pair of dark swim shorts he wore when he worked out.

She turned and sauntered—it was the only word for it, really—to the edge of the pool and dipped her toe in. There would be no stopping her, he could see that. He shrugged his T-shirt over his head. If he were honest, his resistance was at an all-time low. And while he shouldn't want it, the chance to be so near to her, with so little clothing involved, was too tempting to pass up.

And it would give him the chance to watch her face again when she saw his body. In the gym that first day she'd admitted she'd seen enough. He wondered if she would feel that way now.

He looked over his shoulder and watched Katharine, totally focused on the cold water climbing her midsection as she went deeper into the pool, and pushed his pants and underwear down his legs, pulling his swim shorts on before she turned around and was able to see just how interesting a sight he found her.

"Coming?" she asked.

She had no idea how close he was. Rather than offering up that bit of information, he smiled and made his way down to the pool, not wasting time acclimating to the temperature. He lay down on his stomach and pushed through the water. Katharine was still only belly button deep, her eyes round, her nipples beaded tight, and obvious against the tiny triangles of her top.

"Cold?" he asked.

She shook her head. "Not exactly. Feeling a little warm, truth be told."

"Then come in."

"Getting closer to you won't solve my problems."

He straightened, treading water for a moment. "What exactly does that mean?"

She cleared her throat. "Sorry, I'm not very good at this. I meant…being near you, it's what's making me hot. Seeing you like that."

"Like this?"

"Almost naked. That first day…in the gym…you took my breath away."

"My scars did, you mean?" he asked, swimming close enough for his bare feet to connect with the sandy bottom of the pool.

"Your scars are—" she took another step, the water rising higher on her body "—they look painful. In that sense, yes, they are unattractive. But they don't cover up what an amazing body you have." Her cheeks were pink, from the heat or embarrassment, he wasn't sure.

But he was having trouble thinking straight. His body was on fire, his heart threatening to pound straight out of his chest.

"You said you'd seen enough," he grated.

"Only because if I saw more I knew I was…I was going to do something to really embarrass myself. I had never felt anything like that before."

"I thought you loved my brother."

"Not like that. I cared for him. I was sad when he… I was

sad, of course. He was a nice man, and I could have even been happy with him. But I never felt passion for him. I never wanted him. Not like I want you."

"But he was…he did not have scars. And I'm not just talking about the scars on my skin."

"They aren't what I see when I look at you, Zahir." She went deeper and pushed forward, skimming across the surface of the water in a smooth motion, stopping just in front of him. She pressed a kiss to his chest, just above his heart, right by a deep, jagged line of damaged flesh.

"Are you seducing me?"

"Is it working?" she asked, green eyes so earnest it hurt.

"Yes," he said, his voice rough; a stranger's voice. "But you don't know what you're asking for, Katharine. I don't even know."

"I'm showing you that here, in broad daylight, with my full wits about me, that I want this. That I want you. That you're so handsome you take my breath away."

"This is about more than that," he said. "Always, always I have to concentrate. To keep control. To make sure that I don't…miss anything. That nothing happens."

She shook her head, green eyes round. "No. You don't have to. Rest. With me."

One of her legs tangled with his beneath the surface of the water, so cool and smooth. So sexy it sent a shudder of need through him. He wrapped one arm around her waist, drawing her to him, her flesh slick against his, the feeling so erotic he was afraid he was going to lose it then and there.

Right there, those words, they should have made him stop. Should have made him release her. Let her go. Because he had nothing to counter those words with. No offer of a future. She offered him rest, while he could offer…what was there to offer?

She had helped him, it was undeniable. She had changed

him. She had given and given. And he had taken it all. He was about to take more, but if it cost him his soul he could not turn away.

He should. But he could not. She offered him her body, and so much more. Rest. And the need to take it was such that he ached with it.

He lowered his head and claimed her lips, his tongue sliding against hers, the heat that spiraled though his body reckless and needy. Beyond control.

The slick glide of her flesh against him had him hanging on by the very last shred of his control. He didn't even wait for it to snap. He simply let go and fell into the abyss of desire that had opened up in him.

Katharine felt the change in Zahir. His movements fluid, when before they had held tension. His mouth was hungry on hers, his hands sliding over her curves effortlessly, aided by the water.

He cupped her bottom with his large hand, kneading her flesh. She arched into him, unconcerned with the indelicate moan that vibrated through her. Because she couldn't worry about anything except pleasure when Zahir was touching her.

He moved his hand down and gripped her thigh, drawing her leg up, opening her to him. He rocked the hard ridge of his arousal against her and she gasped, tightening her hold on him so that she didn't lose her hold and float away.

"Zahir," she said, knowing he would want to hear it again. And because she couldn't hold it back.

"Did you bring anything? A blanket? I will lay you in the sand if I have to," he growled against her lips, "but I would like something softer for you."

"I brought a blanket," she said, heat creeping into her cheeks.

"Minx."

"You love it."

"I'm not opposed to it."

He lifted her up out of the water and hoisted her into his arms. "In the bag!" she said, pointing to the backpack.

He bent down, still keeping his hold on her, and pulled out the beaded, opulent quilt she'd stolen off her own bed earlier. Folding it small enough to fit in the pack had been a trick, but a trick well worth the effort.

He had to release her to spread it out, and she felt cold, unsatisfied without his touch. As soon as the jade silk was spread out over the soft ground, she dropped to her knees, ready for him. Beyond ready.

He went down with her, on his knees, and he pulled her to him. He didn't ravish her lips like she expected. He paused, stroked his fingers over her face, brushing her hair from her eyes.

"Having limited vision when there is so much beauty to see may be my greatest curse," he said, his voice sounding constricted.

She took his other hand in hers and put it on her waist. "You can use your other senses to help you see," she whispered.

"And I will, *latifa*, my beauty, I will."

He stroked his hand over her hip, then up to her breasts, teasing her nipples. But it was just a stop on his way up to the knot of string that held her bikini in place. He released it with practiced fingers, letting it fall down to the blanket. "So incredible," he said, cupping her skin.

"I feel as though I owe you," she said, putting her hands on his lean hips and hooking her fingers into the waistband of his swim shorts. She tugged them down, the fabric catching on his arousal. She cursed softly and he laughed.

"It's okay," he said, his hands covering hers as he finished removing them.

"Nothing wrong with your body at all," she said, encircling

his length with her hand, squeezing him lightly. Amazing. She hadn't realized just how incredible a man's body could be. How much it would turn her on.

She doubted a random man's body would have half the effect on her that Zahir's did. She was certain, in fact. He was special. He was incredible. And she spoke the words, so he would know.

He caught her hand, stilling her movements. "There still won't be...when Alexander comes of age..."

She looked down, ignoring the sadness that was swelling in her chest. "I know."

"I have nothing for you, Katharine."

She squeezed him again. "That's not true."

He let his head fall back on a groan and he gave himself over to the pleasure she was giving him. It made her heart race. Made her feel a sort of heady rush of power, along with arousal. Making him hot got her hot. His pleasure radiated through her, almost as powerful as if he were the one stroking her.

And then he was, his fingers moving over the fabric of her bikini bottoms before he pushed beneath the fabric, stroking over her damp flesh. She looked at him, met his eyes while they gave and took pleasure that way.

When they were both panting, Zahir untied her bikini bottoms and pressed a kiss to her lips, dipping her gently onto the blanket. He covered her then, his gaze intense on hers. He slid a hand over her body, over her curves, then down in between her thighs.

He stroked her, his touch like fire, a wicked heat that spread through her like flame in the desert. "I have to be sure you're ready," he said, sliding a finger inside her.

She nodded, arching against him, digging her heels into the blanket. He added a second finger, gently stroking in and out of her, the sensation so deep, so intense, she didn't know if she could withstand it.

"I'm ready," she said.

He searched her face, the concern there, on his scarred, warrior's face, so touching it made her heart squeeze tight.

She parted her thighs and he settled between them, the thick head of his erection testing her, pushing in slowly, allowing her time to adjust to having him inside her.

She gripped his shoulders tight, knowing her fingernails were digging into him. Unable to care. But his hoarse groan of pleasure as he thrust into her fully made her think he didn't care, either.

And then she couldn't think at all. Because he was moving in her in the most amazing way, pushing her arousal up another notch. To a level she hadn't imagined existed.

She gripped his back, slid her hands over his skin, feeling the rough, scarred flesh beneath her palms. Her Zahir. She moved her hands down and cupped his butt, drawing him tighter into her, meeting his thrust at the same time, the motion sending a hot pulse of desire through her.

He thrust, and she met him, the two of them creating their own rhythm beneath the hot desert sun.

Sensation built in her until everything in her seemed to seize up for one, immeasurable moment. She wanted to cry out, but she was frozen, clinging tightly to her last bit of control. And then it all burst free, pleasure, satisfaction, pouring through her like a flood, dousing the heat, quenching her thirst.

Zahir felt his climax roaring through him, felt his grip on everything but Katharine slipping, fading. And he wasn't afraid of it. Or what he might do. Because Katharine was precious, amazing. She filled him.

And when he came, he welcomed the hot rush of pleasure that blocked out everything else. The white-hot flame that licked through his veins and jump-started his heart, making it race, filling him with wave after wave of pulsing emotion.

When he finished, he gathered her to him, watched a sleepy smile cross her face, beautiful green eyes closing.

And for a moment, he felt peace.

"It's late."

Katharine opened her eyes, shocked at how cold the air had become, how dark it was. She nestled into Zahir's chest, curling her fingers in.

He picked her hand up and kissed her palm. "Don't you think we should head back, little kitten?"

She laughed. "Kitten?"

"I have the scratches to prove it."

She rolled onto her back and put her hands over her face. "Sorry."

"I'm not."

"Simply incredible," she said, removing her hands and staring at the clear sky. Stars were starting to bleed through, like glittering dust across the vast space.

"The desert is like a different world at night."

She rolled to her side. "I didn't mean the desert. I meant you."

"Katharine..."

"Oh, come on, Zahir, since when does a man reject a compliment in relation to his sexual prowess?"

"It has been so long, I cannot remember what I used to say in response."

Katharine's stomach tightened. She'd wondered if there had been a woman since the attack. Since Amarah.

"It used to be an easy thing. What was a little harmless sex? I was a man with money and power, and women loved that. I wasn't vain but...I was handsome, and they wanted me. It was all so easy."

"You could have still had women, Zahir. You must realize that."

"But why would they be with me, Katharine? For what reason?"

"Pleasure," she said without skipping a beat.

"Maybe. Or would it be because they didn't think they could tell the Beast of Hajar no? That they could not refuse the Sheikh? Before, I never asked why. I just accepted what was there for me. But now…I wonder why they said yes then, too." He laughed. "Being alone gives you too much time to think."

"I don't know why the other women said yes. But I didn't just say yes, Zahir, I said take me. I did it because I want you. You. Not you in spite of the scarring, the ones inside or out. You with the scars. They don't scare me. They don't bother me. I don't find you to be less of a man. I think you're more."

He didn't speak; he simply stared at the sky for a moment. "I kept them away because I feared what I might do. What might happen. But when you touched me this time, I knew it would be all right."

Katharine felt her throat tighten, her chest aching with tears.

"We need to head back now," he said, his voice rough. She knew he regretted being so open with her. But she couldn't regret it. She wanted to hold it tightly to her chest, cling to it.

She nodded. "Okay."

She didn't want to head back. She wanted to stay in their Oasis, with their blanket of stars. Because it was the Oasis of Hope. And she was afraid that as soon as she stepped outside of it, the little kernel of hope that was growing inside her would vanish.

She knew why she'd said yes.

She was in love with Zahir.

The realization made her feel like her heart was going to

burst from her chest. She'd known that being with Zahir ran the risk of heartbreak. But she hadn't imagined this. Being in love with a man who would never want or return the emotion.

# CHAPTER TWELVE

Zahir had slept like hell. Images of Katharine, her body, her scent, the way it had felt to be in her, to have her surrounding him completely...they had plagued him all night long.

And yet it had kept the demons at bay. Unsatisfied sexual frustration was much easier to deal with.

He let the night's dreams play in his mind again. It was only her.

After their time in the Oasis, he had sent her back to her room for the night. Because she'd been a virgin, and he'd been celibate a little bit too long to trust that he wouldn't ask too much of her body.

And because he didn't want her in his bed. Listening to the dreams. Didn't want to take the chance that, if he were too far out, he might lay his hands on her and cause her harm.

But the dreams hadn't come.

He didn't know what that meant.

He stood from behind his desk and stretched his muscles slowly. Bent his knee to make sure it was warmed up. It was always worse after inactivity. And after too much. A tricky balance, but one he had figured out.

He had often thought of his new body as a prison cell. As a place he had been locked in, something foreign, not really him.

It hit him then how untrue it was. He didn't like being

limited. He didn't like looking like a monster, having one eye he could barely see out of. He hated the limp. He hated the flashbacks most of all, though they seemed manageable.

But it was his body.

The moment he had entered Katharine, the moment he had felt the intense wash of pleasure cover him, unlike anything he had ever known, in his life before the attack, and most especially after, he had known. It was his body. Not a place his soul had been locked inside of. Not a prison sentence.

That meant that he never would be released of it. He would never be free. It also meant he had to stop waiting around like he would be someday.

The soft knock at his office door didn't belong to Katharine. He was certain of that. Though, just the thought of her made his stomach clench tight, made his blood rush south.

Rafiq, his chief aide, the man he sent to do most public appearances in his stead, came to him, a broad smile on his face. "Glad to hear the wedding went well. Sorry I couldn't make it."

"It's fine. The birth of your son was more important." Zahir let himself wonder for a moment what it might be like to have children of his own. He had taken it for granted when he'd been younger. Something he would get to someday.

Now…

If he had a baby, it would be scared to look at him. And he wouldn't know what to do with it.

"The people want to see you and your new wife."

"They've been blessedly free of the sight of me for the past five years." His recent drives into the marketplace being the exception. "I doubt they would want it to change now. You know what they say. What they think."

"But they do want to see you. You were in the magazines all over Europe. A royal wedding. The Sheikh and his princess."

"The Beast and his lady? I've seen the headlines. Oddly I've found that if, given the choice between having my scars mocked or romanticized, I would choose being mocked."

"Only you, my friend."

"What are you suggesting I do, Rafiq?"

"You and Princess Katharine need to make a public appearance. A wedding celebration would be ideal. It would make your people feel involved."

"I didn't intend for them to feel uninvolved."

"But they do."

"But that is…"

"Oh!" The sound of shock came from Katharine, who was standing in the doorway looking back and forth between Zahir and Rafiq. "I didn't realize you were busy."

"You mean to say you didn't realize anyone dared breach the inner sanctum? I'm Rafiq, his advisor. Though, I've been gone, as my wife was due to give birth. Sorry we didn't have the pleasure of meeting."

Katharine nodded stiffly. "Nice to meet you."

Rafiq stood, flashed a dazzling smile at Katharine. Even though Zahir knew that Rafiq wouldn't even look at a woman who wasn't his wife, his gut still churned. Rafiq had always been handsome—at least women had always said so. He wondered if Katharine agreed with that assessment.

"I'm trying to convince your husband to stage a wedding celebration for the people of Hajar. Photos of the wedding are all over European news outlets and the people here, I think, feel preference has been shown."

Katharine looked at him, her eyes round. "We can't have them thinking that."

Zahir tightened his hand into a fist. "Oh, no, but do we want them thinking their ruler is a lunatic?"

"You did fine at the wedding," she said.

Rafiq looked at him. "Granted, I haven't been around through all of this. I'm just telling you what I've heard tell of."

For so long, his people hadn't wanted to see him. They had been content to weave a legend around him. Speculate as to whether or not he really still lived, although that fact was easily proven.

Now, though, he felt there was no way to turn his back on the request. Changes had to be made, some already had been. But this would test him. It would test him unlike anything else he'd ever endured since the attack.

But he would do it. He was no longer serving a jail sentence in his own body.

"When shall we plan it for?" he asked.

Katharine looked at Rafiq, then back at him. "I think we could get something together by next weekend if we worked quickly."

"Wonderful," Rafiq said. "We'll plan to have it in the square."

Zahir swallowed hard. The square. The common area of the capital city. Where celebrations were held, where the attack on the royal family had occurred.

But he was done living with fear. He had conquered the wedding. He had made love to Katharine as a man should be able to make love to his wife. He did not fear his own mind, his own body, as much as he had a month ago.

"Then let's start planning."

Katharine's duties in regards to the wedding celebration seemed to consist of little else beyond menu planning and approving designs sent over by Kevin. He was all about transforming her into a hip, modernized version of what he seemed to think a *sheikha* might look like.

The designs were lovely and it had been hard to pick. And the food that she'd been asked to approve was lovely, too. She smiled when she saw Zahir's favorites and hers. She wondered if it was the chef that had remembered, from the night she'd prepared the meal, or if Zahir was the one who had ordered it.

She sighed heavily. Zahir didn't seem to remember she was alive. Or at least that they'd made love. He'd made no move to touch her since they'd been together. She was starting to take it personally. Actually, she'd taken it personally the moment he had walked her to her bedroom and then turned away from her, heading to his own. It was so far from her romantic ideal it was ridiculous.

She blew out a breath. The celebration was tomorrow. She had no idea what Zahir was thinking, how he was feeling. She hadn't realized, when Rafiq had said the square, just what he'd meant. Not right away. And then, listening to talk between the staff, she'd figured it out.

That they would be taking a car right through the part of Kadim where the attack had occurred. That made this more than a showing of love for his people, but a showing of strength. To show that they were not defeated by that tragedy.

She was certain that for Zahir, it was torment.

"He isn't going to come to you and share his feelings," she said into her empty room.

No. If there was going to be any feeling sharing done, she was going to be the one doing it.

She stood from the bed at the same time the door to her room opened. There was Zahir, shirt unbuttoned, hair out of order, his feet bare. "Katharine, tomorrow…I have to be strong tomorrow."

"You will be." Her throat tightened.

"If I am not?"

"I have never seen you be anything less. You have been asked to endure too much in your life."

"But it has been asked of me, so I must go on. And I must do this."

She stepped to him, put her hand on his face, over his scars. She moved her fingers over the parts of his skin that were most affected, the corner of his lip that was tugged down by thick, healed tissue.

Her heart was in her throat, threatening to bring on a monsoon of tears that might never stop. "You will do this, because you are the man who was meant to be here. You are the man who was called to this." She closed her eyes and pressed her lips to his ravaged cheek.

She felt him shudder beneath her mouth and she kissed him again, at the corner of his lips, his jaw, his rough neck.

"Don't, Katharine."

She raised her head. "Don't you want *me*?"

He huffed out a laugh, a tortured sound that twisted her heart, made it feel as though someone had wrung all the blood from it. "How can you want me?"

"Why? Because I'm beautiful? My father sees that as my one credit. He was certain you would marry me because of my beauty. Now, you tell me, is that a credit? Should I feel superior in some way because I was born with good looks? I don't."

"I was born with them, too," he said.

"You still are, you know. Sexy." She put her hand on his chest, pushed his open shirt from his shoulders and let it fall to the floor.

He pulled away from her.

"You are," she said. "Looking at you...it makes me tremble inside. And it's not fear. It's...electric. It's...desire. Need. So deep that I feel like I'll never reach the bottom of it."

She put her hand on his chest again, more firmly this time. Zahir was tempted to pull away again in part. But he wasn't strong enough. He couldn't deny the need that coursed through him.

He took hold of her wrist and pulled her into his body,

capturing her mouth with his, the groan that rumbled in his chest speaking of ecstasy and agony.

Because that's what it was. This driving, intense need for her. It was the greatest pleasure and deepest pain. It forced his heart and soul from behind the protective stone wall that had been forged around them. He felt exposed, and raw. Bleeding. And yet simply too desperate for a taste of her to turn away.

He had to leave the stone walls behind. It was a double-edged sword. If he remained protected, he wouldn't have the pain, but he wouldn't have the full force of pleasure, either. And he burned to experience the pleasure. He couldn't worry about what might happen.

He kissed her with all the desperation of a man who had just found water in the midst of a desert. He was that man. In so many ways, he was that man. He had wandered for years, feeling nothing, thinking he had no need of anything. That he was beyond help.

Until he stumbled upon an oasis. Katharine. His oasis. His hope.

"I need you," he said roughly. He had never spoken words that held more truth.

"I need you, too," she said.

He couldn't fathom it was so. She meant sexually, perhaps. But his words had pertained to something much deeper. Something he couldn't name or understand.

He tugged at the zipper of her dress, but it only moved a fraction of an inch. He tugged again and it remained stubborn. With a feral growl, he gripped the fabric on either side of the zipper and tugged it opposite ways, forcing it open, tearing the fabric in the process.

He let the dress fall to the ground, his body tightening painfully when he saw what was beneath. No bra, and only the tiniest pair of silken panties. Her nipples were pert, ripe, perfect.

He put his hand on her back and pulled her to him, lowering his head so that his lips hovered over one of the rosy peaks. "It seems you bring the Beast out in me," he said, drawing the tip of his tongue around the tightened bud.

She gasped and arched her back, pressing her breast closer to his mouth. "I'm not complaining," she said. "You don't have to hide anything from me."

"A deal." He drew her nipple into his mouth and reveled in the raw sound that escaped her lips. "So long as you hold nothing back from me."

She shook her head. "I won't."

"Lie down on the bed." She complied, backing up to the edge of the bed, her eyes never leaving his. He walked over to the far wall and flicked the lights off.

"No," she said. "Lights on."

He hesitated for a moment before switching them back on.

She smiled like a very well-satisfied cat who knew she'd got her way. "Better," she practically purred.

She sat on the edge of the bed and slid her panties down her legs. And now he was very glad he'd left the lights on. He pushed his pants and underwear to the floor and made a move to the bed.

"Wait," she said. Her skin was flushed, the color spreading from her full breasts up into her cheeks. "I just want to look at you."

He could only look at her, at her perfect body, his heart thundering in his chest, an answering pulse beating in his rock-hard erection.

She pushed back so that she was lying on the bed, reclining against the massive amounts of pillows that were placed against the headboard, her eyes still locked on his. When her hand moved between her thighs his heart nearly stopped.

She bit her lip, a small sound escaping her mouth. "Just

looking at you, Zahir…it's enough to…" She drew in a sharp breath.

Reflexively, his hand moved to his shaft, squeezing himself, trying to get to do something to quell the heavy ache that was taking over his body.

"That's even better," she said.

He watched, held captive, as she moved her fingers over her own body, her eyes never leaving him. She was breathing heavy, her nipples tight, her stomach expanding and contracting sharply with each breath.

She raised a hand to cup her breast and his heart nearly stopped before roaring on at twice its normal rate.

He squeezed himself again, this time in an effort to slow things down, to keep himself from ending things before he even got to touch her, as she was touching herself.

"Are you going to come over here?" she asked, her voice breathless, speaking of her arousal.

"You don't have to ask twice." He moved quickly to the bed, placing his hand over hers, on her breast and at the apex of her thighs.

She smiled and removed her hands, letting him pick up where she'd left off. He took her nipple between his thumb and forefinger and tugged slightly, finding his reward in her tiny gasp.

He moved his fingers between her delicate feminine folds, finding them slick with her arousal. He moved his hand over her there, in time with his movements on her breast.

She gripped his forearm, her head falling back, the flush in her skin deepening. Not embarrassment, like he'd originally assumed. From desire.

"Zahir, now. Please."

He changed positions so that he was on his knees before her and hooked her thigh over his hip, thrusting into her as he pulled her against him. His growl of pleasure was met with an emphatic sound from Katharine. She rocked against him, knowing the right rhythm to please them both.

He flexed his hips and took himself deep and she arched back into the motion, gripping his forearms. He held on to her tight bottom, holding her steady, making sure every thrust counted.

He felt her internal muscles tightening and releasing around him, knew she was ready to go over the summit, and he felt an answering wave of sensation wash through his body. He quickened his pace.

He looked down at her, her lips parted slightly, her eyes clouded with pleasure, watching him, looking at him with such...trust.

His heart seized tight along with the rest of his body and as his orgasm crashed through him he felt his heart open up, spilling emotion into his chest as he lost himself in her.

It was as though everything—ecstasy, despair, darkness and light—had all descended on him at once. Crowding in on him. Threatening to overwhelm him.

So he looked at her face and rode out the storm with her, not looking away until the fire in him had ebbed to a slow burn.

Even in the aftermath, he kept one hand on her cheek, her cool, smooth skin his anchor. Because everything else in him had changed in a monumental way. And he didn't know what it meant. If it meant anything.

The only certain thing was that tonight he was sleeping with Katharine in his arms. Where she belonged.

Where he belonged.

He smoothed her hair back, kissing her forehead. "It is true that you are beautiful," he said softly. "But it is not your beauty I need. It is you."

\* \* \*

He opened his eyes again when the morning light was shining through the windows. He had slept. And he remembered nothing of it. No images. No dreams. Nothing but sleep.

He looked at Katharine, curled up next to him. Last night had been…he didn't know. But something had changed.

Today was the wedding celebration. And he wasn't filled with dread. He felt new. He didn't feel the old claws digging into his back, reminding him that he might fail. He would succeed. He would do it for Hajar. For Katharine.

He just would.

Today, failure was not an option. And he suddenly realized that hiding in his palace, avoiding failure, too afraid to face the unknown, had been failure in its own right. He hadn't seen it that way, and now it was so clear he couldn't understand how he'd missed it.

He wanted to wake Katharine up. Just to tell her. Because only she would understand. He touched her shoulder and she shuddered beneath his hand.

"Zahir," she whispered. "No!" She rolled over and sat up, her breath coming in deep, gasping sobs, her frame shaking.

"Are you all right?" he asked, putting one hand on each of her shoulders, bracing her.

"I'm…oh…I had a horrible dream. Like you said. All the people…darkness. It was…" She put her hand on her chest, her fingers trembling. "You're safe, though." She swallowed. "That's good."

He took his hands off her. Guilt tugged at him, twisted his stomach into a knot. What had he done to her? What had he put inside her head? He had slept, and she had endured his torment.

He swallowed the bile that was rising in his throat.

"Get dressed. We have a long day ahead of us." He looked at her face, her lovely green eyes, always so expressive, clouded by fear.

He tightened his hands into fists and stepped away from the bed, reaching down to collect his pants from the floor. "I'll see you later," he said.

She nodded, drawing the sheet up to her chest. He turned and left her there, his heart raw and wounded in his chest.

# CHAPTER THIRTEEN

"Don't worry, I put on lots of sunscreen."

Zahir turned and saw Katharine walk into the palace entry-way. One pale shoulder was revealed in its entirety, the other covered with a gauzy swath of beaded fabric in a deep green that complemented her ivory skin and pale, strawberry hair.

Her arms had been inked with pale, rust-colored henna, her hands and palms too, decorated with winding vines and flowers, traditional for a Hajari bride. It looked so exotic on her, even to him. Even when he had seen it done on many women before her, on her it seemed unique, special.

"I hope you did," he said. With her arms and shoulders on display she would need protection against the hot sun. "I hope you had it on that day at the Oasis."

She blushed slightly and, for a moment, he was amused that she could still blush. "I did. If I hadn't, you would have known, because I would have resembled a radish by day's end."

He looked at her for a moment, awed by her effortless beauty. She might not imagine it to be a great asset, but he was certainly captivated by it. Although, that was not everything.

"You are beautiful, Katharine. But it wasn't your beauty that made me say yes to the marriage. It was your argument. The fact that you knew what you wanted, what you needed, and set out to get it. I respect that."

Katharine felt tears building in her eyes. She swallowed hard. "Thank you."

"It is the truth." He shrugged and turned away, his manner stiff.

He'd been acting strangely since that morning. But then, the last time they'd made love there had been no morning after at all, so this, at least, was better than days of nothing.

"Well, I appreciate hearing it." She studied his profile, the straight set of his shoulders. "You're okay." It wasn't really a question. She could see that he was.

"This is a celebration." He turned to face her, the cold light in his dark eyes making her stomach tighten. "Let's go celebrate."

The limo drove up through the crowded center of the square. The crowd of people was firmly behind the barricades, and security was out in the front and back of the car. Everything was safe and secure. Still, Katharine watched Zahir for signs of tension, her heart racing, her palms damp with sweat brought on by intense nerves.

Nothing could be more terrifying for him than this. Nothing would ask more of him. And every fiber of her being was rooting for him. Because he could do it. He was the strongest man she'd ever known.

"What happens now?" she asked as the limo eased into a vacant spot behind a massive stage area that had been set up near the back of the square.

"I'm giving a speech."

"In front of everyone?"

He offered a halfhearted grin. "The hazards of political living."

"And you're doing it now. Living politically, I mean."

"It's what I'm meant to do."

Her throat tightened and she offered him a smile, the best

she could manage with tears threatening to form. She nodded. Because there was nothing she could say. She was too filled with pride, overwhelming emotion, to speak.

The driver came around to the side of the car and opened the door and Zahir slid out then turned, extending his hand to her, "Come with me?"

She took his hand and allowed him to help her from the car. She squeezed his hand, and he led her up to the stage. The roar of the crowd was like a hive of bees on a grand scale, and it made Katharine feel dizzy. Celebrating in Hajar was louder than it was in Austrich. She liked it. So much unrestrained joy, and all directed at Zahir.

"You go," she said, when they got to the foot of the stairs.

He looked at her and released her hand, continuing to the stage on his own. Katharine watched, everything in her feeling tight, making it hard to breathe.

As soon as Zahir ascended to the podium, the crowd went silent, all eyes trained upon the Beast of Hajar.

Zahir spoke in Arabic, and Katharine called on all that she'd learned of his language, both during her engagement to Malik and her stay with Zahir.

"For too long, there has been a dark cloud over our country. Some might say, I was the dark cloud. But it is no more. We are a strong country, a strong people. We all lost much on that day, when our liberty, our happiness, was attacked. But we have emerged stronger. Yes, we have wounds to show for it." A small cheer erupted at that and Zahir pressed on. "But we are stronger for them. And we will move into the future, never forgetting those who were lost, but never forgetting to live. For we have been given a gift. We live on. And the important thing now is what we do with that life. That is something I learned from your new *Sheikha*, my wife, Katharine Rauch."

Katharine was wiping tears from her cheeks when Zahir

gestured for her to come up onto the stage with him. She blinked and tried to swallow the aching lump in her throat as she ascended the stairs, waving at the crowd of cheering people. Her people.

Zahir took her hand in a display of solidarity and the crowd grew louder. And Zahir stood strong. A man ready to rule his people in a new way.

He had walked up onto that stage as the Beast and he was leaving their king.

The entire vibe of the Hajari wedding festival was different from the pomp and circumstance that their Austrichan ceremony had possessed.

She had really enjoyed the spa-style preparations. A bath with scented, spiced oils and floating jasmine blossoms, hot wax on her hands and feet to make them soft. And then the women had spent hours working on the detailed henna artwork that decorated her arms and hands.

They were gorgeous, but her favorite designs were the ones they had added to her feet, spiraling up her legs. For the Sheikh, one of the women had said with a very knowing smile.

Katharine had a feeling the Sheikh would like very much.

The buffet was being served, more food than Katharine had ever seen, and people were eating and laughing. So many people had come. It was a healing for the nation, and for the nation's ruler.

And her heart felt like it would burst with happiness.

Entertainers came and performed for them. A band and a belly dancer. The woman was like a siren, long dark hair swirling over her barely covered breasts, her hips moving in sensual time with the music. It was almost as though she was directing the band. As though her body commanded them.

Katharine leaned into Zahir, who was seated next to her,

placing her hand on his thigh beneath the table. "How about if I learned to dance like that?"

He turned his head sharply, his expression fierce.

She smirked. "Not in front of other people. For you." She let her fingers drift over his thigh, up higher.

"That has possibilities."

"I thought it might."

She loved that she had power over his body. So much strength, so much man, and he responded to her touch. An amazing, heady feeling. One that made her feel good. Not lacking. Like she was just enough.

"I think it is time I was alone with my bride," he said.

She knew that tonight she was going to get her wedding night.

Back in her room, she lit every pillar candle she could find, placing them on tall, ornate stands. It bathed everything in a sensual, flickering glow. Perfect for what she had in mind.

Zahir was already lying on her bed, his focus on her. He looked relaxed, but she knew differently. Every one of his muscles was tight, ready to spring into action at any moment. Ready to pounce on her.

Not a bad idea at all.

She couldn't get enough of him.

"Dance for me now," he said, his eyes dark, glittering in the firelight.

She smiled and swayed her hips to the side. "Like this?" For some reason, she had no inhibition with Zahir. He made her feel…like herself. Just Katharine. For the first time in her life.

"More."

She shimmied again and then laughed. "Okay, I have no rhythm."

"You have fantastic rhythm. You may not know how to belly dance yet, but you have fantastic rhythm."

She reached around behind her back and unzipped her dress, watching his face closely. Everything in his face tightened, the tendons in his neck standing out when she let the dress fall to the floor and she revealed the extent of the henna artwork that covered her body.

Vines climbed her legs, creating a provocative look that drew his eyes. And she knew he couldn't look away.

"You want me, right, Zahir? Not just any beautiful woman?"

He rose up to his knees. "You are my *latifa*, my beauty. Katharine, it is more than just simple skin. Beauty is much more complex than that. It is you, you alone, I want. My body had not responded to anyone sexually in years. I didn't know if I had lost that part of myself, too. A drive completely erased from me. And then there was you. But I was afraid…afraid of what losing control might do to me. But when I lose control with you, there is only freedom. There are millions of beauties. But you are the only one my body desires."

He moved to the edge of the bed and encircled her waist with his arm. He leaned in and pressed a kiss to the henna blossom on her thigh, then traced it with his tongue.

"Come, *latifa*, let me show you how much I desire you."

And as he kissed her, entered her body, he whispered words meant only for her ears. Meant only for her, pleasure raining on her like a shower of sparks, a warm, honeyed feeling began to spread through her. Something beyond the physical, something beyond her love for him, even.

Acceptance.

"Katharine," he whispered.

And in that moment she felt very much as if she had to do nothing to be enough. With Zahir, she simply had to be.

* * *

"Zahir."

She called out to him in her sleep again. Zahir watched as Katharine's brow wrinkled and her body shook.

She was scared. For him. Of him. It didn't matter.

Tonight, there had been bliss. He had forgotten, for a moment, seeing her in the throes of her nightmare that morning. He had forgotten all that something like that meant.

It wasn't simply that she was having nightmares; it was the effect his darkness was having on her bright soul. She had brought light in, and he had polluted it.

He put his hand on her face and she quieted. And his heart clenched tight.

That emotion that had hit him last night, again tonight when he'd entered her body, it was back. Truthfully it had never left. And there had been hints of it long before he'd ever made love to her.

He loved her. With every shred of his broken soul, he loved Katharine.

He would give his everything for her. It would never be enough. Not while the trade-off was nightmares and sadness. His own demons now circling her in her sleep while he took comfort in her arms.

It was sick. It was selfish. He would take the flashbacks, the pain and fear, the anger, all of it back, if only it wouldn't plague her as it had him.

How could he keep taking from her while he made her ill with his past? That he would send her torment, when she had offered him rest.

He could not do that to her. Even if what he had to do would kill the new life that had just started to grow in him.

When Katharine woke the next morning the bed was cold and the candles had burned down on their stands into wrinkled, misshapen masses.

Zahir was standing with his back to her, his focus on the scene out the window, the sun rising, turning the air around them orange.

"Every morning I am thankful I did not lose my sight in both eyes," he said.

Katharine sat up, letting the bedcovers fall around her waist. "Every morning?"

"There is not a day when I don't think about it. Not a day when I don't realize how much more could have been lost to me." He turned to face her. "It would have been a shame, never to see your face."

His voice sounded strange, guarded. He reminded her more of the man she'd first met rather than the man she'd gone to bed with the night before.

"If you wish to go back to Austrich, you are free to go." The words were stark, random. Painful.

"What?"

"I do not need you here. When we first struck this agreement, I thought that I might. But…you have made your appearance. Of course, you will need to come back periodically, but my people will understand that with the failing health of your father, you have duties at home."

Katharine felt ill, like she'd been punched…no, it was deeper than that. As though she'd been flayed, gutted, everything in her pulled out, leaving nothing but raw, bleeding confusion.

His people. Not hers. Not theirs. Last night she had felt a part of Hajar, and of him. Now he was drawing a line. There was no malice in his voice, not anger or hate. Just a simple, matter-of-fact statement.

"What happened to…everything you said? I… Do you want me to go?"

"We've had… It's been good between us," he said, his eyes flickering back to the sunrise. "But I have responsibilities here and your presence has been…a disruption. I need to be able to concentrate. To keep a handle on everything."

Now anger flared inside of her. He may feel nothing. Blessed, empty nothing, but she felt everything. And she refused to keep it inside. "A disruption? Is that what you call it? As if I was no help to you? What about yesterday?"

He swallowed. "Yesterday would not have played out as it did if I hadn't married you. Cause and effect. Anyway, I had thought you were hoping to conduct as much of the marriage as possible from Austrich."

"That was before."

"Before sex? You instigated it, I assumed you wanted it. It was never meant to change anything. It didn't change anything. You knew that."

There was no response to that. Because she had. In her head, she had. But her heart had forged a connection with him, one she'd been so certain he'd felt, too.

The things he'd said…

She shook her head, getting out of the bed, using the sheets as a cover. "It changed things, Zahir. It did. Five years without a woman, remember? You told me I was different."

A muscle jumped in his jaw. "You are."

"Then what is this?"

"I am giving you your freedom!" He roared the words, the Beast in him surfacing, a side of him she had nearly forgotten existed. "I am offering to let you out. To give you all that you asked for from day one! Why do you fight me?"

"Because I've changed," she said, her throat tightening. "My feelings have changed. You…you showed me things about myself. You made me believe that I could just be me."

He shook his head. "No. Do not speak."

For once, she heeded his command, because she couldn't have formed words to save her life. Her throat burned, her eyes aching to spill the tears she was forcing herself to hold back.

"I do not want to hear about your *feelings*," he said, his voice harsh. "They have no meaning to me."

"Yes, they do. I know they do. I remember last night, what you told me. That I was your hope. And I believed…"

"You are right," he said, his voice low and rough with emotion. "I said those things. I meant them. You are brilliant, Katharine, a shining star. All any man could ever want in a woman. But I am dead inside. I feel nothing," he bit out. "And you deserve a man who can feel everything."

She swallowed, trying to force the motion when her throat was blocked by a lump that made her ache and burn.

"Since when is it up to you to tell me what I deserve?" she said.

"Why will you never stop trying to force yourself into my life!" he roared.

"Get out," she choked, shocked by his words, numb to her core, little flashes of pain breaking through the blessed fuzz, giving her hints of just what she was in for later.

He didn't move, he only stood there, watching her. For what? For a crack in her armor? To see the effect of the devastation he had just poured over her?

"Out!" she said again, her voice breaking.

He inclined his head and walked out. His steps were heavy, his walk uneven, familiar. She felt a tear slide down her cheek and she brushed it away, turning her back on him until she heard the door close.

She walked into the bathroom and dropped the sheet, leaving it bunched around her feet.

She leaned over to the mosaic-tiled shower and turned the water on, waiting until the spray was hot before getting in and standing beneath the punishing heat.

She looked down at her arms, at the henna designs still

inked into her skin. A sob climbed her throat and she grabbed a bar of the luxurious handmade soap set in its gaudy golden holder and rubbed it over her skin, trying to remove the marks.

Trying to erase him. What she had done for him.

It wouldn't come off.

She dropped it onto the floor of the shower and lowered her head, letting her tears blend in with the water that was cascading over her hair. For one moment, she imagined boarding a plane and going back to Austrich. It had been home all of her life. She could go back, live in her father's house. She had withstood his cutting remarks all of her life. She had remained strong. She still could.

But that thought only lasted for a moment.

She looked back down at her arms, at the vines and flowers, still so vibrant and strong, even beneath the elements.

Her heart felt as though it was going to burst with the pain it was in. With the brutal force of his rejection.

But the henna remained. It had been a symbol of their marriage. The sand remained, too. As did the change he had brought about in her. The belief that she was worthy. That she was worthy on her own. Without having to earn it, or prove it. It was a part of him he had left behind. The grains of sand that were embedded in her, impossible to remove completely.

The vase of sand that had been created on their wedding day. It had been unwelcome then. A shocking surprise that seemed so out of place with their fake arrangement.

It hadn't been. It had been true. He was a part of her. He had been then. And she knew, beyond anything, that she was a part of him. He might not believe it, but he was.

More likely, he knew it, and he couldn't face it.

She put her hand over her face and wiped the water and tears away. She wasn't going back to Austrich. It wasn't an option. Quitting wasn't an option. Turning away from the man who had shown her her own inner strength, who believed in that inner strength, wasn't possible.

She owed both of them more than that. She knew now that she owed herself more than she'd been ready to give. That she deserved love. And that Zahir could give it to her. That no matter what darkness or fear held him back, it was there.

He should know her well enough by now to know that *Sheikha* Katharine S'ad al Din would not back down from a challenge.

Zahir felt like he was bleeding inside, and he didn't know how to staunch the flow. It was pure pain, hot and destructive.

Letting her go was bad enough. To have to hurt her to have it done was unbearable. This was a the kind of pain a man could lose himself in.

But theirs was an imbalanced relationship. She gave and she gave. And he took it all. And he relished it.

He strode out of the palace to the paddock. He could not watch her leave. He knew she would, he had made sure to strike at her, to hurt her as best as he could. He closed his eyes, let all of the emotions wash over him, let them tear through him like a tidal wave. He waited for something, for the flashbacks. There was nothing. Nothing to cushion the pain. Nothing to take him from this moment.

He saw Katharine's face. And he felt like he had finally found himself again. But it hurt like hell.

But he couldn't watch her leave. That he could not do. Because he would stop her.

He prepared Nalah for the ride, all of his usual survival gear in place in saddlebags. He had to get away. Because his strength would only last so long.

Watching her go would break him. He had rebuilt himself once. He did not know if he could do it without her.

# CHAPTER FOURTEEN

ZAHIR's hand shook as he placed it flat on the door to what had been Katharine's bedroom. He had been gone three days. Long enough to give her a chance to get her things together.

Things would settle in. They would have to. She would get over feeling hurt. She would be relieved eventually. If her father died, he would fulfill his duties as much as was needed, even if it was just on the legal end. Katharine hardly needed him to hold her hand. She was strong. Stronger than he was. Stronger, smarter, than anyone he'd ever known.

He debated whether or not to open the door. Whether it would be too final. If he left it closed, perhaps he could still imagine her there.

He shook his head. No. One thing he didn't do anymore was ignore pain. Or feeling. She had taught him that. Had helped him find his heart again.

He pushed the door open and his heart seized tight.

There she was, sitting on the edge of the bed, her posture stiff, her hands folded in her lap, her jaw set.

"What are you doing here?" he asked.

"Oh, I didn't leave," she said.

"I asked you to."

She nodded. "You did. And then I told you to get out of my room, but here you are."

"Three days later."

"Still."

His throat felt tight, far too tight. "Why are you here?"

"Because I'm not leaving. I committed to that the very first day, and I'm standing by that. I'm not leaving you. Not until we speak with some honesty between us."

"You should," he ground out. "You…what can I give you, Katharine?" The words were torn from him, from his heart and not his mind. "You have given and given, and I take and take from you. Why do you accept it?"

"Because I love you."

He felt the words hit him like a physical blow, spoken so soft, so sweet, with the power to drop a grown man to his knees.

He shook his head. "You cannot."

"Why? Because you have scars? Don't you realize that I…"

"Because of who I am," he bit out. "What I am. To heal myself I have stolen light from you and I cannot bear that."

"Do you know what I see when I look at you, Zahir? You are the bravest, most amazing man I have ever known. You have conquered more than any one person should have to take on, and you have done it with so much power."

"I have been afraid…"

"Good," she said, a tear sliding down her cheek as she stood. "Good. Because that tells me that you're even braver. Because you do it anyway. You think you take from me? Don't you realize what you give me? Respect. Caring. You're the only person in my life that has ever seen me as more than just looks. More than a pawn. You told me you would have thrown me out that first day if not for my actions. If not for my words. Not my body. Not my connections. How can you not know what that means? What's that done for me?"

"The people in your life have been fools, Katharine. You are beautiful, the most beautiful woman I have ever seen. But it's your heart, your character, your mind…that is what

I...I see your face. When memories or nightmares crowd in, I see your face and it banishes the darkness." He took a step toward her, cupping her cheek with his hand. "But I fear I have left the darkness with you. You are everything good and bright, and I have tainted you with the death that lives in me."

She shook her head. "Why would you say that?"

"You had those dreams. I...I could not bear to continue poisoning you."

"Zahir...yes, I had some bad dreams. About losing you. That happens when you're trying to hold on so tight to something, and you fear it might slip away. It's what happens when you fear you're in love alone. It's not you. There is no death in you. No darkness. You have given me more joy, more happiness, more pleasure than I've ever had in my life. You haven't stolen my light from me. Light banishes darkness, Zahir. It wins. All you have done is strengthen me."

He believed her. Her words filled with such strength and conviction he would be shamed to call them lies. The truth in them rang down to the depths of his soul. "But I am not... I'm not everything you should have. I am not even near what you deserve."

"And I'm probably not everything you should have, but that's not how it works. I love you. And with that, I take everything you are. And if you could love me, too, you'd take all of my bad things along with the good."

He looked at her, at the stubborn set of her chin, so familiar, so precious beyond words. And he felt hope break through. Happiness, love, filling him. Things he had thought lost to him forever. "Like how bossy you are."

She frowned. "Yes."

"I accept that." His heart felt like it started beating again after being stopped for too long. Like he was truly alive after being dead for the past five years. "Everything about you. Because I love you, Katharine."

"Zahir…you…you told me you didn't love."

"I didn't go in crowds, either. There were a lot of things I didn't do before you. A lot of things I did not believe were possible for me to do. I know why I love you. You brought light into my world, you changed me." He put his palm flat on his chest, felt his heart thundering beneath it. "Made me move forward. It's easy to love you. You made me feel at home in this body. I haven't felt home for five years."

Katharine let out a watery laugh and wiped at tears sliding down her cheeks. He moved in, eyes locked with hers, touching the wet trails on her cheeks. "What I don't understand is why you love me," he said.

"That moment when the paparazzi were at the gate, and you walked out and faced them head-on, I knew what sort of man you were. I knew the strength of your spirit. I've seen you do the honorable thing time and time again, even when it cost you. You stood up to my father, and you told him without any doubt that you saw more in me than simple beauty. And before all that I saw your amazing body." She laughed again and it forced a smile to curve his lips, made some hope pierce his chest. "I don't want anyone else, or another version of you. Just you. Not the man you were, the man you are now."

"You helped me become that man. You helped me fight what I could not fight alone."

"We'll do that. For each other. For the rest of our lives. Some things will be too big for me to face alone, and I know when that moment comes, you're the one I want fighting at my side."

His throat tightened and harsh breath escaped his lungs. "It killed me to send you away. But I thought…I thought it was what I had to do."

"Oh, Zahir." She wrapped her arms around his neck and held him. Then she turned her face and pressed a kiss to his scar-roughened cheek. "That's why I love you," she whispered. "Because you would have done that to yourself to try to save me."

She pulled her head back and looked at him. "But don't ever do anything like that again. You broke my heart."

Katharine felt the last bit of pain inside her melt away as she looked into Zahir's face. As she saw every emotion written clearly and honestly on his face.

"I broke my own," he said. "I didn't think it was possible. I thought I had no heart to break, but you destroyed every barrier I had placed around my heart. You have made me new. I was lost, in my pain, in my sorrow. You pulled me out. I didn't know that I'd been living in hell until you showed me what else I could have. Until you showed me that I had let part of myself die. You brought me back."

Katharine looked at him, at her warrior sheikh, the man who had endured unspeakable loss, the man who had hardened himself to the point of being unreachable, and she saw the glitter of tears in his dark eyes.

It was her breaking point, and she let her own tears fall. "I really do love you," she said. "All that you are. All that you have become. The good, the bad and everything else."

"As I love you," he said.

"Even when I'm bossy?"

He encircled her with his arms and pulled her into his body. "Especially when you're bossy." He captured her lips with his, and she poured all of her love into the act, drinking in every bit of it he offered back until she was filled with it.

"Come with me," he said, twining his fingers through hers and leading her out of the room and down the long corridor that led to his wing of the palace.

"You're not going to continue living down the hall from me, are you?" she asked.

"No. I do not sleep without you. I cannot."

"Well, good. I don't sleep well without you, either."

He led her into his bedroom and she felt fresh tears when she looked and saw what was sitting on the vast mantel across from his bed. Their wedding sand.

"Even though I had sent you away," he said, his voice rough, "I could not forget this. I could not stop feeling how true it was. I put it here after I got home, just before I came to see you. I knew that no matter how many years passed, the truth of it would remain. You are in me, a part of me. Always."

"And you're a part of me," she said. "A much loved part."

"We will tell our children this story."

She felt her heart swell. "Children? I thought…"

"I never truly feared my children crying at the sight of me. But I was afraid…I was afraid I would not be able to love a child. Because I had lost so many of my emotions. I don't fear that now."

"We'll tell them all about the princess and the magic sand," she said, smiling through her tears.

"But there was no magic," he said. "It all came from the princess. From her strength, and her cleverness. And from the love she showed to a Beast."

She stood up on her toes and pressed a kiss to his lips. "Now that's a fairy tale."

He brushed her hair away from her eyes and she looked at the man she loved. At a face that spoke of pain, but that had grown more precious to her than any other sight she could imagine.

"A good thing," he said. "Because I know for a fact that we'll live happily ever after."

\* \* \* \* \*

# REQUEST YOUR
# FREE BOOKS!

## 2 FREE NOVELS PLUS
# 2 FREE GIFTS!

PASSION
GUARANTEED
SEDUCTION

---

**YES!** Please send me 2 FREE Harlequin Presents® novels and my 2 FREE gifts (gifts are worth about $10). After receiving them, if I don't wish to receive any more books, I can return the shipping statement marked "cancel." If I don't cancel, I will receive 6 brand-new novels every month and be billed just $4.30 per book in the U.S. or $4.99 per book in Canada. That's a saving of at least 14% off the cover price! It's quite a bargain! Shipping and handling is just 50¢ per book in the U.S. and 75¢ per book in Canada.* I understand that accepting the 2 free books and gifts places me under no obligation to buy anything. I can always return a shipment and cancel at any time. Even if I never buy another book, the two free books and gifts are mine to keep forever.                    106/306 HDN FERQ

| Name | (PLEASE PRINT) | |
|---|---|---|

| Address | | Apt. # |
|---|---|---|

| City | State/Prov. | Zip/Postal Code |
|---|---|---|

Signature (if under 18, a parent or guardian must sign)

Mail to the **Reader Service:**
**IN U.S.A.:** P.O. Box 1867, Buffalo, NY 14240-1867
**IN CANADA:** P.O. Box 609, Fort Erie, Ontario L2A 5X3

Not valid for current subscribers to Harlequin Presents books.

**Are you a current subscriber to Harlequin Presents books
and want to receive the larger-print edition?
Call 1-800-873-8635 or visit www.ReaderService.com.**

\* Terms and prices subject to change without notice. Prices do not include applicable taxes. Sales tax applicable in N.Y. Canadian residents will be charged applicable taxes. Offer not valid in Quebec. This offer is limited to one order per household. All orders subject to credit approval. Credit or debit balances in a customer's account(s) may be offset by any other outstanding balance owed by or to the customer. Please allow 4 to 6 weeks for delivery. Offer available while quantities last.

**Your Privacy**—The Reader Service is committed to protecting your privacy. Our Privacy Policy is available online at www.ReaderService.com or upon request from the Reader Service.

We make a portion of our mailing list available to reputable third parties that offer products we believe may interest you. If you prefer that we not exchange your name with third parties, or if you wish to clarify or modify your communication preferences, please visit us at www.ReaderService.com/consumerchoice or write to us at Reader Service Preference Service, P.O. Box 9062, Buffalo, NY 14269. Include your complete name and address.

HP11B

The scandal continues
in The Santina Crown miniseries
with *USA TODAY* bestselling author

# Sarah Morgan

Second in line to the throne, Matteo Santina
knows a thing or two about keeping his cool under
pressure. But when pop star singer Izzy Jackson
shows up to her sister's wedding and makes
a scandalous scene that goes against all royal
protocol, Matteo whisks her offstage, into his limo
and straight to his luxury palazzo…. Rumor has it
that they have yet to emerge!

# DEFYING THE PRINCE

**Available August 21 wherever books are sold!**

www.Harlequin.com

HP13090

*Harlequin® Romance author **Barbara Wallace** brings you a romantic new tale of finding love unexpectedly in* MR. RIGHT, NEXT DOOR!

*Enjoy this sneak-peek excerpt.*

"IT's TOO BEAUTIFUL A DAY to spend stuck inside. Come with me."

"I can't. I have to work."

"Yes, you can," Grant replied, closing the last couple of steps between them and tucking a finger underneath her chin. "You know you want to."

"So, you're a mind reader now?" The response might have worked better if her jaw weren't quivering from his touch.

"Not a mind reader," he replied. "Eye reader. And yours are saying an awful lot."

His touch was making her insides quiver. She wanted desperately to look away and refuse to make eye contact with him, but pride wouldn't let her. Instead, she forced herself to keep her features as bland as possible so he wouldn't see that a part of her—the very female part—did want to go with him. It also wanted to feel more of his touch, and the common sense part of her was having a hard time forming an opposing argument.

"If so, then no doubt you know they're saying 'remove your hand.'"

He chuckled. Soft and low. *A bedroom laugh.* "Did you know they flash when you're being stubborn?"

Rather than argue, Sophie swallowed her pride and looked to his feet.

"You so don't want me to move my hand, either."

"You're incorrigible. You know that, right?"

HREXP0912

"Thank you."

"I still want you to move your hand."

"If you insist…." Suddenly his hands were cupping her cheeks, drawing her parted lips under his. Sophie's gasp was lost in her throat. As she expected, he tasted of peppermint and coffee and…and….

And, oh wow, could he kiss!

It ended and her eyelids fluttered open. Grant's face hovered a breath from hers. Gently, he traced the slope of her nose and smiled.

"Your eyes told me you wanted that, too."

If she had an ounce of working brain matter, Sophie would have turned and stormed out of his apartment then and there. Problem was one, she was trembling and, two, the fact she kissed him back probably wiped out any outrage she'd be trying to convey.

So she did the next best thing. She folded her arms across her chest and presented him with a somewhat flushed but indignant expression. "Do not do that again."

*Will Grant convince Sophie to let her guard down long enough to see if he's her MR. RIGHT, NEXT DOOR? Find out in September 2012, from Harlequin® Romance!*

Harlequin®

# SPECIAL EDITION

**Life, Love and Family**

*NEW YORK TIMES* BESTSELLING AUTHOR

# KATHLEEN EAGLE

**brings readers a story of a cowboy's return home**

Ethan Wolf Track is a true cowboy—rugged,
wild and commitment-free. He's returned home to
South Dakota to rebuild his life, and he'll start by
competing in Mustang Sally's Wild Horse Training
Competition.... But TV reporter Bella Primeaux
is on the hunt for a different kind of prize,
and she'll do whatever it takes
to uncover the truth.

## THE PRODIGAL COWBOY

*Available September 2012 wherever books are sold!*